WOMAN ON THE EDGE

WOMAN ON THE EDGE

•

JOANN SANDS

AVALON BOOKS
THOMAS BOUREGY AND COMPANY, INC.
401 LAFAYETTE STREET
NEW YORK, NEW YORK 10003

PRINTED IN THE UNITED STATES OF AMERICA
ON ACID-FREE PAPER
BY HADDON CRAFTSMEN, SCRANTON, PENNSYLVANIA

To my brother, David Renninger
and
his lovely wife, Kathy

''Who can find a virtuous woman?
For her price is far above rubies.''
—Proverbs 31:10

Chapter 1

As Valerie Quinn stood by the counter trying to decide the type of doll a five-year-old would prefer, she was unaware of the malevolent eyes watching her from the gift section of the pharmacy. She was much too involved with her shopping to feel the piercing gaze on her back. And too, it was the season of peace and goodwill—a time when one put personal grievances behind and tried, if only for a short time, to get along with everyone.

Valerie loved dolls, she always had. Even now it was hard to walk by the doll section of a gift shop and not stop to look. But look was all she could do, for it was difficult to splurge on nonessentials when her own fledgling business was not quite off the ground yet. Someday she would be able to purchase a couple of quality dolls to sit around her shop. One of Cinderella or Rapunzel—fairy-tale dolls, imaginary characters who had helped her through the trauma of her bruising childhood. Whatever would she have done without the companionship of her dog-eared storybooks or hand-me-down teddy bears? But never many dolls. The only new one she ever had went up in flames.

Valerie pulled off her brown driving gloves so she could handle the doll better. How mature they were making them, complete with a tiny waist and a swelling chest. Laying it down, she walked farther down the aisle. A "little girl" doll was more in order for Megan. Yes. A doll with a child's figure under a cotton dress . . . a plaything with ribbons in her hair, that's what Val herself would have wanted. And since Megan had blond hair, she would probably relate best to a dolly who had the same. That finally decided, she reached for the object at the precise moment another did.

But that second hand drew back abruptly. Valerie wasn't sure if it was to allow her to have the toy or to cover his mouth as he sneezed; she suspected it was the latter.

"God bless you," she said, turning, and the smile on her lips froze. Gilbert Ellis! He was the very last person she wanted to see, and from the awkward expression on his face, she knew the feeling was mutual. Still, he managed a haggard smile.

"Hi, Val. I didn't expect to see you here."

Obviously, or she knew he would have ducked down another aisle. They'd been avoiding each other for weeks. For a moment, they stared into each other's faces, not knowing quite what to say, but knowing they had to say something. And the funny way things have of working, the next moment, they both said in unison, "Are you ready for Christmas?"

A ripple of exchanged laughter relieved their tension before Valerie replied, "I'm not. Each year I promise myself I'll start earlier and each year it's the same old story. I'm still doing serious shopping the last full week of Christmas.

I'm planning to stop in at Alexandra's this evening, so I wanted to take a gift along for Megan. How about you?''

"I still have a few on my list. I came in here for something for my niece."

"Elizabeth? Gil, she's around eleven now. I'd think a Walkman would be more appreciated, or one of her favorite videos."

He smiled sheepishly. "That goes to show you how much I know about . . . " The rest of his sentence was lost in an explosive sneeze. "I'd better stock up on some antihistamine while I'm here. Then I hope the citizens of this town behave themselves so I can spend a quiet evening at home."

At that moment, a boy rushed by, knocking Valerie off balance. Gil reacted quickly as he reached out to steady her by the shoulders. And once again, their eyes locked uncomfortably. His gaze wandered to the lustrous auburn hair she held in place with a large barrette, to her slightly upturned nose and kissable lips. And then on to the open leather coat which didn't quite hide her appealing figure.

Darn it all! He didn't expect to feel this way around her. He certainly didn't want to! His cheeks flushing deeply, he felt a bit light-headed. Gil told himself it was the fever, but he knew that wasn't entirely true. That old sadness of heart touched him again and he wished vainly that he had his years after graduation to live over again. Given the chance, he would never have lost touch with this woman. He drew in a deep breath and the words came rushing out before he could stop them. "Val, is there any chance of you . . . "

"No."

"No?" He arched a sandy brow. "What do you mean, no? You haven't heard the question yet."

Reaching up, she disengaged his hands from her shoulders. "I don't have to, Gil. I know exactly what you're going to say. I didn't think it was a good idea a few months ago when you asked me and I still don't. There are other interior decorators you can hire. Just consult your Yellow Pages.''

''You're that busy, huh?''

''Well . . . '' she hedged. ''No.''

''Really, Val, at this stage of the game, I don't think you should be so quick to turn down a prospective client. Times are tough and you could do a lot worse, a whole lot worse. For one thing, I'm easy to please and for another, I pay cash, so you won't be stuck.''

He could see her weakening just a little. ''It's a big house, Val,'' he pressed a bit more, ''and all ten rooms need extensive work.''

''I don't know, Gil. I'm an engaged woman.''

''So? You mean you won't take on any single male clients?'' he asked, a twinkle of amusement in his eye. ''What are you afraid of?''

''You're being ridiculous.''

''And you're being obstinate. Come on now, admit it. This project will pay your rent for months to come.''

Valerie smiled sweetly as she folded her arms across her chest, determined to get the best of him yet. ''I won't be living in rent much longer. I'm getting married soon, or haven't you heard?''

''How soon?'' That twinkle was gone.

''The date isn't definite, but it will be sometime in the spring.''

''It's him, isn't it? He won't allow you to work for an old boyfriend.''

''Geoffrey has nothing to do with it. It's my choice and I choose to avoid the hassle of taking you as a client. Believe me, it's better this way.''

''Val, if you needed my professional help, I'd give it to you.''

"You're a public servant, I'm a businesswoman. There's no way you can equate the two," Valerie reminded him as she turned to leave, the box tucked under her arm. "Goodbye, Gil."

"No, wait a minute." He hesitantly touched her sleeve and his happy-go-lucky facade dropped away to reveal a very sedate young man. "I'm sorry. I promised myself when you became engaged to that baby doctor, this would never happen again. I know in my head you're off-limits, but making my heart accept that, well, it's not quite that simple. Now, don't say anything," he was quick to add, seeing she was about to. "I'm . . ." He sneezed again, then smiled thinly. "I'm getting my cold medicine and leaving before I manage to stick my other foot in my mouth. I probably won't see you before Christmas, so you have a good one."

"You too, Gil," she said, watching him turn and walk down to the over-the-counter medication aisle. For three years they'd been high school sweethearts, then career choices sent them on different paths. She hadn't seen him for the past nine years until their chance meeting in a restaurant back in June. That's when he told her he had applied for a job with the local police department and, if he got it, he'd move out of Philadelphia and into Cedarcrest. He'd asked her if it was okay if he called for a date. The prospect excited her, but he never did phone. And in the month that followed, she began to date one of her clients—Geoffrey Faraday. By the time Gil finally got around to her, she was too much involved with Geoff to care that he didn't contact her because of indifference, but rather because of his involvement in undercover work. Now he was in town to stay and he was living in the old Victorian house she had wanted to buy.

Deep in thought, Valerie walked right by the person who'd been watching her with hateful eyes, never once sensing the ill-willed intentions. She continued to the counter, and after paying for her purchase, she had the clerk wrap it. While she waited her gaze dropped to the dwindling stack of the town's weekly newspaper, *The Cedarcrest Gazette*. Gil's picture appeared on the front page. Of course, one would never know this was Lieutenant Ellis, local hero, for he was dressed as a woman . . . a decoy out to nab the man coined the Shopping Center Mugger, who was preying on the senior citizens. Things had gotten mean, and after an attack which left one woman with a fractured hand and another suffering from a coronary in the aftermath, the residents were up in arms, complaining bitterly that the police weren't doing enough to protect them. Gil requested to be assigned to the case and when the mugger struck again, he was surprised to find the stooped, layer-clothed old woman wasn't at all what she appeared. Before the culprit knew what hit him, he was lying face down in the snow with his hands being cuffed behind. A passerby, who had been fortunate enough to choose that particular area to take winter photographs, happened to swing around and snap a few of the action as well. Gil had tackled the assailant as they were rolling in the wet snow. No wonder he had a cold!

Valerie smiled in spite of herself. One of the reasons Gil had left Philadelphia was to work in a quieter, less crime-ridden community, but he was finding that Cedarcrest had its share as well. She felt a confidential pride in him. The senior citizens could now cash their checks and do their shopping a little more securely, though she knew they'd probably never feel quite as secure as they once had. Being a victim did that to you.

In some ways, Gil had changed a lot in the intervening years, but not at all in others. He now reminded her of a young version of the actor Ryan O'Neil. His blond, wavy hair was shorter and a shade darker than it had been, and his husky frame had slimmed down a bit, but he was the same impulsive personality she remembered. Valerie used to find his outlandish antics amusing. Now she found them annoying and some of the schemes he employed to try to woo her back into his life both embarrassed and infuriated her. Like the time he hired a small plane to fly over her street on her birthday, trailing the banner, VALERIE, I LOVE YOU. And she, thinking this unsigned declaration was from Geoffrey, called him at his office. Geoffrey assured her he would never do anything so tacky as that. Of course she should have suspected Gil all along. Wasn't he the one who spray-painted their names on the bridge when they were both seniors? And it remained there until the structure was repainted only last year.

''Here you are, Miss,'' the clerk said, handing her Santa Claus motif package back. Valerie thanked the woman, then turned and walked out of the drugstore.

While Gil was waiting for his purchases to be tallied, he turned at the sound of Val's high heels echoing against the tile floor. He'd figured the only way to forget her was to totally avoid her. But how do you successfully pull that off when you both reside in the same small town? They were bound to run into each other occasionally. Had he only not bought that aging Victorian over on Reed Avenue. They were both present at the auction and when he and Valerie were the last two competing, he got carried away, bidding against her on a house he didn't really want, but knowing she did. It was his last and costliest venture to win Valerie back. Too late, he finally understood what his father tried to impress upon him all along: you cannot buy another's love. He reluctantly bowed out to Geoffrey Faraday, accepting him as the one who conquered Valerie's heart.

The scowl on his brow deepened. Was she ever really his? At one time he had thought so, but looking back now, he wasn't so sure. There was an air of mystery about the girl which his own parents were sensitive to, even if he wasn't. His minister father had skillfully though unsuccessfully tried to draw her out during an evening meal. Val refused to discuss her childhood. It was as though she were a woman without a past. But she would talk eagerly to him about her aspirations of becoming an interior decorator. While his mother warmed to Val, he was well aware of his father's reservations. And though he had her to his home often, she never invited him to her apartment. There were always excuses. Lately he wondered about that. All he knew was she had been raised by her widowed mother, a woman he never met. Amazing, he thought. How could you date someone for three years and never know her parent? When he asked about the mother during his recent chance meeting with Val, she'd simply said her mother had passed away a few years ago, but didn't say why; and he didn't ask, though he was curious. He was curious about a lot of things now that he was trained to detect and analyze—not the least of which were those scars across her . . .

Gilbert sneezed hard.

The salesclerk looked up as she handed him his purchases. "Take care, Lieutenant, and have a nice day."

Though he wished her the same, he wondered how he possibly could, as lousy as he felt. He couldn't wait to get in bed and begin an uninterrupted night's sleep in that creaking old empty house he now called home.

Gilbert never noticed the person who'd been watching Valerie first, then him. So he never suspected that a cold with its accompanying chills and fever was the least of his worries now.

Valerie and Alexandra Baxter became fast friends from the time they met at Geoffrey's Labor Day pool party. At first, she didn't want to attend, feeling she'd have nothing in common with the friends of her pediatrician client, but he persuaded her to come, insisting everyone wanted to meet the interior decorator who'd done such a magnificent job turning the antique showroom into a charming sunroom and gallery. No one seemed to be surprised when their professional relationship evolved into a personal one. And when Geoffrey gave her a diamond on Thanksgiving Day, their friends shared their happiness. Valerie felt she was the solution to a widower's loneliness and his five-year-old son's rowdiness. Ryan clearly needed someone to step in and take over in the area of discipline, but in her private moments, she wondered if she were the one. There was no chemistry and the bonding she was hoping for never came.

The stalker sat in the truck, watching Val and gathering the nerve it took to do what had to be done. A hand slid under the blanket and touched the gun. The bullets were in the chamber and the silencer was in place. The breath drawn in was a deep one. *Do it! Do it now while she's in the open.*

Rolling the window down, the perpetrator had a clear view of the victim now. Easing the gun out of its conceal-ment, a shaky hand brought it up, then froze at the sound of the wail of a siren piercing the silence and of the flashing red and blue lights lighting up the darkness.

Do they know? Could they possibly know? Did that cop notice the surveillance in the pharmacy after all? It would be like Ellis. Got to get outa here. . . .

The stalker was about to put the pickup in first when the patrol car whizzed by, its driver never taking his eyes off the speeder down the road. With gaze shifting once again to the apartment, the stalker saw Valerie disappear into the fashionable brick building.

Shoulders slumped, but heart still racing, the pursuer

gripped the wheel. *Maybe it's for the best. This might need more thought. Perhaps she should be toyed with like a cat would torment a mouse . . . and give her a good scare while I'm at it. Yeah.* A cruel smile appeared beneath the beard, and the eyes, which usually were kind, revealed signs of near madness at that moment. The heartbreak, hopelessness, and hatred had taken possession and became all-consuming.

When Megan Baxter answered Valerie's ring, the child's face broke into a wide grin. Her eyes were focused on the package tucked under the woman's arm.

"Is that for me?"

"What? No hello or come on in?" Val encouraged the bright-eyed little girl in a very grown-up–looking denim skirt and vest ensemble.

The child stepped aside and before she could answer, her mother called out from the kitchen. "Who is it, Meg?"

"Val. And she brung us something."

Alex came into the living room, wiping her hands on a terry towel which she then tossed over the shoulder of her Atlantic City sweatshirt. Her long blond hair lay in a single plait, draping her left shoulder, and as usual Valerie thought she looked more like a coed than the editor she was for *The Cedarcrest Gazette*.

"Hi, Val. You timed this rather well. I just placed the scalloped potatoes and meat loaf in the oven, and it's more than we can eat."

"Thanks for the invitation, but I can't stay."

"You can stay long enough to take off your coat, can't you?"

"I suppose." Val laid the gift on the coffee table and removed her gloves. As she slipped out of her coat, Megan leaned over to look at the name tag. Her face lit.

"It says TO MEGAN. It is for me! Can I open it?"

Val looked over at Alex, who nodded. "Knowing my daughter as I do, we'll have no rest if I say wait."

That was all the invitation the girl needed. The wrapping was off in a jiffy, and when she looked through the clear covering over the face of the box, her expression registered no disappointment. "Oh, she's so pretty! And she's got hair the color of mine. Thank you, Val."

"Now that that's over with, have a seat, Val, and explain to me just why you can't stay. Didn't you tell me Geoff's attending a seminar?"

"That's right. He'll be spending the night at some plush center city hotel with his colleagues, so I intend to spend a quiet evening at home pampering myself with a bubble bath, a pedicure, and then I want to curl up with a sizzling romance I bought at the supermarket."

"I would say that romance is one thing that's not lacking in your life these days."

Val laughed, then, not giving Alex a chance to quiz her, changed the subject. "Are you ready for vacation?"

"I'm getting there. Mom and Dad have been wanting us to visit them for months now and I think it's about time I take them up on it. It's giving me something to look forward to after Christmas. The holidays are especially hard with John gone. You're not too surprised when a seventy-five-year-old has a heart attack, but when a thirty-seven-year-old does, it really knocks you for a loop." Then the young widow laughed nervously and gestured with a waving hand. "Enough of this melancholy chit-chat. Now I want to hear about you, Val. Have you decided where you're going on your honeymoon?"

"Paris. Geoff's never been there."

"And you?"

"Me? Oh my, Alex, I've never been anywhere worth mentioning."

"But all that's going to change. Geoff will see that you make up for lost time."

Val agreed, then looked toward the child now sitting on the stool by the Christmas tree, examining her new doll. Alexandra watched a dreamy smile spread across the face of her younger friend and she wondered about her. Valerie's past was somewhat of an enigma to her, which aroused Alex's natural inquisitiveness. Even now, she couldn't help but be curious about certain things—like those scars on the backs of her hands. She asked Valerie once and she replied with a quiet, "I cut them." which was evident, but the how and the why wasn't. The scars weren't really disfiguring, though they were noticeable. Alex noted that Val sat, one hand on top of the other, palm side up, self-conscious of the only flaw in an otherwise lovely woman. *What is she thinking*? Alex pondered, watching Val watch Megan. That smile had now been replaced with an expression of longing and near-despair. *Looks like I'm not the only one who gets despondent around the holidays*, she mused and was about to ask if she was all right, when Megan spoke.

"Mommie, can I give Val her present now too?"

"I don't see why not, honey. Go ahead."

She leaned over, knowing the box by its wrapping beneath the brightly lit tree, and carried it over to Val. "Here, this one's yours." And she stood right there, anxious to watch her open it.

Valerie tore the holly print wrapping off with almost as much enthusiasm as the little girl had. As a child, she never received many gifts. In the beginning, she thought she'd misbehaved somehow . . . that Santa was angry with her. It wasn't until years later that she could finally admit her mother was too uncaring to spend money on such trivials as toys.

Val removed the lid and laid the tissue paper back. Inside

was a pair of smart driving gloves. Eagerly, she dug her hands into them.

"Do they fit?" Megan asked, still hanging close to her.

"They're perfect!"

"I helped Mommie pick 'em out," she informed her with a note of pride in her voice. "Do you like 'em?"

"Oh yes, honey, I do. Thank you so much." She leaned forward to hug the girl, an embrace which was reciprocated. Then, breaking away, she reached in her purse, drew out an envelope, and handed it to Alex. "Since this seems to be the time to exchange gifts, here's one for you too."

Alexandra accepted it with a "thanks." As soon as she opened it, Megan was quick to ask where the gift was, not seeing a box. "It's a gift certificate, Megan, to the Petite Boutique."

"Get yourself a new swimsuit, or whatever else you need to take along to Florida," Val instructed. "And have yourself a great time. Put aside the headaches at the office and enjoy your family. You deserve it."

Misty-eyed, she reached over and clasped Valerie's still gloved hand. "You're so sweet, Val. It's little wonder that Geoff chose you."

Valerie walked carefully across the parking lot, mindful of the occasional patches of ice, residue from the recent melting then freezing snow. It was six o'clock. She knew this without checking her watch, for the church up at the intersection was playing carols promptly at that hour and now they were beginning to play "Silent Night." Her biggest concern was what to give Geoff, the man who truly had it all. She had bought brass bookends shaped in the form of a caduceus for his den. But she had to get him something really special. A new medical bag perhaps? One with his monogram. She'd take special note to what his present satchel looked like, but knowing Geoff as she did, it probably was in mint condition. Both Geoffrey and his possessions were polished and above criticism.

Arriving at her car, Valerie inserted her key in the lock.

"Hey, Katie!" The driver called out in a voice which was deep and muffled.

Valerie turned to tell him he'd made a mistake, that she wasn't this Katie he took her to be. She didn't recognize the old pickup, nor the bundled driver. But she did recognize the flash of shining metal which suddenly appeared from the window.

The frightened young woman raised her hand in a pleading manner of useless defense. "No! Please don't!"

There was a simultaneous bang and exploding glass behind her. Then the truck sped away and melted into the flow of traffic. The only sound once again was the carillon playing the familiar carol that suddenly seemed so incongruous in view of what had just occurred.

It was at that point that Valerie became aware of a burning pain near her shoulder. Tearing her eyes from the vehicle she was trying to commit to memory, she forced her gaze down to her arm.

A small gasp escaped her lips. A trickle of blood was seeping through the hole in her leather coat. She had been shot!

Chapter 2

Gil rummaged through the dresser drawer for his heaviest pair of flannel pajamas. Finding them, he hastily pulled on the striped bottoms as he talked to the dog, who sat on the braided rug at the foot of his bed.

"What does that baby doctor have that I don't, Brutus? I have a sturdy home to offer Val, though not an estate with a cutesy name attached to it like he does. Stoneybrook. Humph! Sounds like a dorm cabin at a boy's camp. And as far as vocation goes, I'm a professional man too. As long as there are criminals, I'll have work, and we both know, there will always be criminals," he said with a rueful smile.

"If Val thinks it's glamorous being a doctor, she can just think again. When it comes down to the nitty-gritty, you're working with sick, hurting people, and in his case, it's little kids who can't understand their pain. I've been on the scene right after an accident, or confronted an abusive parent who left their kid in a coma. It's not a pretty sight and I don't

15

envy Geoffrey trying to put them back together again. Geoffrey!'' he repeated, uncharacteristically critical, egged on by the negative effects of his cold and his feelings of inferiority. ''Why must that guy be so fancy and spell his name with a *G* instead of a *J* like all the other Jeffreys I know?''

He went on enumerating his peeves as he slipped into his pajama top. The dog sat quietly by, obedient and loyal to the man who used to handle him on the K-9 Unit.

''Faraday might make more than I do, but money's not everything. Granted, it goes a long way. He'll always be able to buy Val stuff I can only dream about. But there's one thing I'd never be deficient in giving her, and that's love. Right, Brutus?''

The German shepherd offered one solid bark. Gil grinned. ''Thanks for your vote of confidence, buddy. You and I always did think alike.''

Feeling a tad better for verbally venting his sentiments, if only to a pet, Gil sank on the edge of his bed and read the directions on the box of cold remedy. He took the recommended dosage with great gulps of water, then lay down to wait for it to take effect. As Gil stared up at the high, artery-cracked ceiling, watching the reflections of the car headlights go by, he decided he must have caught this one the day he nabbed that mugger. After rolling in the snow tackling that guy, he had sat around in wet clothing too long. It was the first time he'd worn all that paraphernalia since his decoy days, working an assignment in Fairmont Park. His smile of satisfaction turned into a sneeze.

The dog jumped, started from his stretched-out, jaw-resting-on-the-paws position. Gil glanced over at him, then closed his eyes and quietly waited for sleep to overtake him. He felt lousy and he could only hope the mugger was feeling the same. The traffic outside gently lulled him to sleep. His last conscious memory was hearing the big brick church on the corner announcing the sixth hour by playing "Silent Night."

The ringing of the phone by Gil's bed interrupted his sleep. Groaning, he reached for the receiver and knocked over the half-full glass of water in the process.

Grumbling a few choice words, he groped to turn on the night table lamp to see what he was doing. The sudden bright light hurt his eyes for a moment and he shielded them as he once again fumbled for the phone.

"Ha-low," he said nasally.

The person on the other end hesitated. "Gil?"

"Speaking." He recognized the voice of the dispatcher. "You'd better have one heck of a good reason for disturbing my sleep, Annie, after I distinctly told you I didn't want to be interrupted."

"There was a shooting outside the Reed Avenue Apartments."

He couldn't remember a day in Philadelphia where there wasn't a shooting, but here in Cedarcrest? It was thankfully an unusual occurrence. "Conway's on duty. Can't he handle it?"

"Yes, and he is, but when he saw who the victim was, he thought you'd want to know."

She hesitated a moment and Gil rolled his eyes toward the ceiling and mentally counted to five. "Annie, I'm in no mood for guessing games, so you'd better just come right out and tell me."

"Valerie Quinn."

A second or two passed before the name really sank in. Now he rolled up on his elbow and his "what" was scarcely more than a hoarse whisper.

"Apparently Valerie had been visiting her friend, Alexandra Baxter. She's the one who made the call and took her into the apartment to wait for help. Miss Quinn seemed to be in a state of shock, so Conway couldn't get much out of her. He's going over the scene now to see . . . ''

"Annie," he cut in, "just how bad is it?"

"I'm not sure."

"Where is she now? Memorial?"

"Yes."

That was a good sign. The really serious cases were taken by MediVac to the trauma center thirty miles away. Holding the phone in position by a raised shoulder, he was already unbuttoning his PJ top. "You did the right thing by calling me, Annie. I'm on my way."

As Valerie lay on the table, she fought back tears more of anxiety than of actual pain. That was behind her now, at least until the Novocain wore off. She was glad it was Doctor Cantrell who was suturing her up; he was considerate of her fear. He'd been speaking to her, but what he'd said was lost in the muddle of her cluttered mind. She tried to make a conscious effort to stop dwelling on the unbelievable events of the past hour and concentrate on what he was talking about.

His eyes flickered up from her outstretched arm to her face and he repeated, "You're Geoffrey Faraday's fiancée, aren't you?"

She nodded. Geoff! Good heavens, what would he say when he heard about this!

"I thought I recognized you. Geoff introduced us when we met at the reception over at the country club. Remember?"

"Yes. Your wife said she was so happy that he finally met someone."

The physician grinned. Tall, thin, and graying, he resembled a model for a Norman Rockwell painting. "That's Nellie for you. Always was a mother hen, always will be. Never mind the fact she's got a brood of six of her own to concern herself with. Seriously though, I'm happy for Geoff too. He's had too much tragedy in his life lately. It's about time something good happens to him."

That's it, doc, keep talking, Valerie urged in her thoughts. *Give me something else to think about besides what you're doing to me.*

"Then there's Ryan. A boy that age needs a mother to look after and guide him . . . give stability to his life. When death takes a parent, especially suddenly like it did his mama, it traumatizes a child and leaves him uncertain and fearful about the future."

You don't have to tell me, she thought. *I've been there.*

"Shall I tell the nurse to have Mrs. Baxter notify Geoff?"

"No. He's in Philadelphia attending a seminar on infant death syndrome."

"Yes, of course. The topic would be of special interest to him. He's a good doctor, Val, but sometimes I think he tries too hard, cares too much. He hasn't really accepted the fact he can't save them all, and when death comes to a colleague or friend, it's especially hard to take. It hurts the old ego, but we don't have the final say when a person's time is up. Fortunately, it wasn't your time tonight. You're one lucky lady. There now, all finished," he announced, tearing off his gloves as he went to the sink. "I'll give you a prescription for pain, though I don't think you'll need it. Have Geoff keep an eye on that, but there again, I don't anticipate you'll have any problems."

After the nurse helped Valerie on with her blouse, Cantrell continued. "The police will want to speak with you now. We're not busy tonight, so you just stay in here where you can talk privately."

As he turned and left, Valerie felt a sinking sensation.
The police? But she had talked to someone named Conway
back at the apartment. Or maybe he had spoken to her. She
did little more than answer in monosyllables as she clutched
the washcloth Alex had pressed to her wound. Well, she
supposed she'd have to talk to this Conway again, not that
she could tell him much. Trying to sift through the fog of
her thoughts, she did sense that he was a patient and com-
passionate man. Maybe it wouldn't be too bad, though her
greatest desire was to forget the whole episode.

Sitting erect on the table, with her legs dangling over the
side, Val tried to prepare herself for the barrage of questions
he would be asking. Only it wasn't Conway who entered
through the curtain. Her stomach fluttered and she blurted
the first thought that hit her.

"What are you doing here, Gil? You're supposed to be
home in bed."

"When I'm told you've been shot, nothing short of being
comatose is going to keep me there." Out of uniform and
dressed in leisure clothing, he walked over to the table and
stood before her. It was hard to be professional when his
personal life was touched. And it was a struggle not to lose
his temper with her cold greeting . . . with the person who
did this to her . . . with someone.

"Are you all right?" he asked bluntly.

"Yes."

"Good. Then you'll be able to answer a few questions."

"I already talked to Conway."

"You didn't tell him anything, Val. You were either too
frightened or hurting too much to offer any details." He
removed a pen and pad from the inside pocket of his jacket.
"Ms. Baxter said you left her place around six. She heard
a 'pop' and the sound of breaking glass—thought it was
some kids throwing a bottle at a sign, but when she looked

out the window, she saw you clutching your arm and leaning against the car. Who did this to you, Val?''

Valerie slid off the table. She was beginning to feel shaky again, but her nervous, pent-up energy made sitting impossible. "I don't know."

"Can you give me a description of the vehicle?"

"It was a pickup truck; an old American model . . . probably a Ford or Chevy."

"Color?"

"Dark."

"Dark what? Green? Blue? Black?"

"I'm not sure, just dark."

"You didn't happen to see the license, did you?"

"Not clearly, but it wasn't an out-of-state vehicle. There was no plate on the front. I believe it ended with the numbers 26. That stuck in my mind because it's my age."

He made a few notations in his little notebook. "All right. What about the driver? Can you describe him?"

She began to pace. "The image that comes to mind is, he was wearing a beard . . . light. And there was light shaggy hair hanging out from beneath his stocking cap. He was wearing glasses too. It's obvious he didn't want to be recognized. It all happened so fast, Gil. Faster really than it's taking me to tell you about it."

He began writing once more. "Did he speak?"

"Yes."

Gilbert looked up, surprised. "Oh? What did he say?"

"He said, 'Hey Katie,' then he squeezed the trigger."

" 'Hey Katie?' " he repeated. "Why not, 'Hey Valerie?' "

Val shrugged. "You're the detective, Gil. Apparently this is a case of mistaken identity. That parking lot isn't very well lit. I suppose I could have resembled this . . . this Katie person."

He didn't look very convinced. "I know this is going to sound strange, but I have to ask anyway. Can you think of anyone who would want to see you dead?"

The young woman flinched. "No. I haven't any enemies, Gil, and I've given no one reason to hurt me. I don't understand. Why . . . why would anyone do this?" she stammered, as she brought a finger to her lips to steel herself.

The officer reached out and laid a sympathetic hand on her shoulder. He wanted to draw her into his arms, to comfort this woman who had been so unjustly singled out, but he didn't dare. He only gave her a moment to compose herself before he continued. "I know this next question is going to sound even more off the wall, but you understand, I must look at every angle. Val, could you have witnessed something that might have been incriminating if you weren't 'dealt' with?"

"No," she instantly assured him.

"Okay, I suppose that's it for now." He put his notepad and pen back in his pocket. He'd been on the force long enough to know that some kooks really didn't need a reason to do what they did. They just chose their hapless victims at random. But why "Hey Katie"? It didn't gel.

"Maybe," he said at last, "Maybe it's as you say. You're a victim of mistaken identity."

"What are your chances of getting him?" she asked directly.

"With a bit of luck, pretty good. Conway's questioning the residents in the neighborhood now. Perhaps someone saw something even more conclusive and will step forward. After all, when the bullet shattered your window, it had to draw attention. You've given us something to go on—more actually than I expected. Eyewitnesses aren't always as helpful as you might expect, especially when they're staring down the barrel of a gun. And that's all they see—the weapon looming before them. You've got an eye for detail. I suppose that comes from being a decorator." Gilbert glanced around and it suddenly hit him. "Where's Faraday?"

"At a seminar."

"He doesn't know yet?"

She shook her head. "There's no need to disrupt his evening."

"Disrupt his evening?" he repeated, incredulously. "Val, you were shot, for pity's sake!"

"It's only a flesh wound," she insisted. "Tomorrow's soon enough. Besides, there's nothing he can do that hasn't already been done."

He zipped his jacket up. "I spoke to Alex a little while ago. She asked me to bring you back to her place for the night."

"That isn't necessary."

"Look Val, you've got a choice," he said, irritable with this woman who was so obstinate. "You can either spend the night with Alex, or come to my home."

Her mouth slid open. "Gilbert Ellis, stop treating me like a child."

"Then stop acting like one. It's not good for you to be alone at a time like this."

"Why? Do you actually think he'll strike again?"

"No, but I do think the full brunt of this hasn't hit you yet. You might want a listening ear and a little TLC."

"Which Geoff can give me when he returns."

"You need companionship now, not tomorrow. Look, the more I consider it, the more I think I ought to take you to my place. Brutus can keep you company until I get the paperwork down at the station house completed."

She shook her head. "You amaze me, Gil. You never,

never miss an opportunity to take advantage of a situation, do you?''

His cheeks flamed, and for the first time since he'd received Annie's call, he was aware of the aches and stuffy head. He clamped his lips shut, fearing he'd only blurt something out he'd later have to apologize for. He should have let Conway handle the case by himself, he really should have.

When Gil dropped Valerie off at Alexandra's apartment, she found the mother and daughter weren't alone. Corinne Greer was there.

Oh great! Val thought. She wasn't up to company, not even the company of a mutual friend.

The attractive raven-haired woman was sitting cross-legged on the floor with Megan, with a well-worn child's board game between them. She looked up now, concern replacing the smile which had been there when she saw who'd just entered. Rising to her sneakered feet, she brushed the seat of her tight-fitting blue jeans. ''Val, are you okay?'' she asked directly.

''I'm fine now. I suppose you heard?'' she asked guardedly as her eyes shifted to the child. The little girl was watching her with an uncertain look on her face as she cradled her new doll. Val placed her overnight bag beside the sofa. Gil had stopped at her apartment long enough for her to gather a few personal items and to change from her ruined blouse to a more presentable long-sleeved jersey.

''I happened to be driving by on my way to pick up some milk and bread at the store,'' Corinne began to explain, ''when I saw all these flashing lights in the parking lot. You know my inquisitive nature, Val, so I hurried here to find out what was up from Alex. You can't imagine the shock when she told me it involved you." Her voice dropped to a whisper. "It must have been horrible."

Valerie nodded mutely as she turned to face the child, who had now conquered her shyness about approaching her. When she had seen her adult friend last, Megan knew she'd been hurt somehow, for she's seen Val's blood-streaked arm and her quiet tears. The curious child had been ushered out of the room when the ambulance arrived. But she stood behind the kitchen door she'd opened just a crack, so she could watch the drama unfolding before her. She heard words like *shot* from strangers, but for some reason, Val seemed more concerned about the new gloves which had been soiled. Alex had told Val they were replaceable, that Val should try to lie still so the paramedics could do their job.

Megan's eyes fastened on the sleeve. "Are you really okay?" she queried in a small voice.

Stooping down to get eye-level with the child, Valerie placed her uninjured arm around the girl's waist. "Yes, honey, I'm really okay, and I'm very sorry if I scared you."

Alex came out of the kitchen, wiping her hands on a towel. Valerie rose, a smile spreading over her face. "It seems we've played this scene once before this evening."

"Only this time you are staying for supper. No arguments allowed." She greeted Valerie with a light embrace, then stood back a pace to survey her. "You're looking much better. The color's returning to your cheeks." Alex nodded to her daughter. "Meg's already eaten, but the rest of us haven't. I've kept it hot, so let's eat, girls, I'm famished."

While Valerie had been friends with the two women a relatively short time, they had known each other for nine years. Alex had told her that she, Corinne, and Geoffrey's late wife Jessica were sorority sisters, although Jessie and

Corie's friendship went back to their childhood. While Alexandra was the only one of the trio to use her degree in journalism, she felt Corie was the most talented of their inner circle. Because of Corie's photographic memory and steady nerves, Alex told Val that she would have made a grade A investigative reporter. But Corie settled instead to be the receptionist/bookkeeper in Geoffrey's growing pediatric practice. No one could have been more surprised than Val when she, who never really felt she was accepted or belonged, found herself replacing Jessica in the clique. At first, she knew they were doing this for Geoff's benefit to please him, but now she felt there was a true camaraderie between them. Her conscience pricked her when she remembered she was disappointed to find Corie there. Of course she would be.

Corinne took charge of the conversation during supper, deliberately avoiding the events of the evening, conscious of the listening ears of the child in the next room. Corinne offered to tuck Megan in bed. When she returned, she commented how much she loved kids—that they could wrap her around their little finger and make her do just about anything . . . especially the likes of Meg and Ryan. Val knew the mood was soon to change and when Corie sat down, it did.

"I'm glad you decided to spend the night with us," her hostess said, taking a slow sip of coffee. "Gil and I discussed it and we both agreed, it wouldn't be wise for you to be alone. At the very least, you'd lie awake in that little apartment of yours, staring up at the ceiling, replaying the shooting over and over in your mind."

Corie rose and walked over to the counter to cut another wedge of pie. "Have you notified Geoff yet?"

Val hesitated, staring at her own piece of half-eaten dessert before answering a quiet, "No."

"Don't you think you should?"

The young woman sighed wearily, her eyes lifting to her friend across the round table. "Oh Alex, if I call him now, he'll come rushing home when it isn't necessary. I'll tell him tomorrow when I see him."

Corie licked the whipped cream off the tip of her thumb as she rejoined them at the table. "I know Geoffrey very well, and believe me, he's not the kind of man that appreciates having things withheld from him. He likes to be up on what's going on at all times, so I'd advise you to tell him before he hears it from one of his colleagues, or worse yet, sees it splattered over the front page of the newspapers."

Valerie laid her fork aside, not able to take another bite. She turned her worried eyes on Alex. For some reason, that thought hadn't entered her mind. "You wouldn't do that, would you, Alex? I mean, give it coverage?"

Alex hesitated, torn between knowing this is the stuff that sells newspapers and understanding it would hurt her friend. "Okay Val," she relented. "But I have no control over what Dr. Cantrell might say, or the folks the police questioned this evening."

Corie was thoughtful as she slowly ate her whipped cream–laden pie. "Did you get a good look at the guy?"

"I did, but he was pretty well disguised." She touched the bandage through her sleeve. "I suppose I am lucky to be here talking about it."

Corinne surveyed Val for a moment. "Maybe not. Maybe he just wanted to scare you good. He must have been close enough to get off a deadly chest shot, yet he hit your arm. It might have been a scare tactic," she repeated.

"If that was his intention, he succeeded."

Alex sat her fork down and gave Corinne a disapproving look. "I think we ought to talk about something more pleasant now."

"Why? It's not going to go away. Besides, for Valerie's own well-being, she shouldn't pretend it didn't happen, because it very well might happen again."

"I agree with Corie, Alex, he probably will attempt it again. But not on me. I didn't get to inform you yet, this whole incident is a case of mistaken identity. He thought I was Katie."

Their "What?" was chorused in unison.

"He said, 'Hey Katie,' right before he squeezed the trigger. I wasn't his intended victim, and he surely realized that at the last second. That's why I wasn't . . . killed." The final word stuck in her throat.

Alex slumped back in her captain's chair. "Well, what do you know. I suppose we should be relieved."

"Is there a Katie living in this building?"

"I really can't say. I've only lived here myself for the past five months."

"We have to find out."

"And just what are you planning on doing, Val, canvassing door to door? And if you find out there is, then what? Are you going to scare some family half out of their wits by telling them some crazed madman is out to shoot her?" Alex's hand closed over Val's wrist and she gave it a light, imploring squeeze. "You're normally a very rational woman, but not tonight. Tonight you're letting your emotions dictate your actions. Not that anyone could blame you. Leave any investigating which is to be done up to the police. They're the experts."

"All right, I'll concede in this instance that you're the one whose thinking is sharper. But I simply can't shake this feeling that Katie's in terrible danger, and if I hear that he does eventually get her, I'll have a real hard time dealing with it."

"If it were me, Alex, I'd want to be told."

Alexandra's mouth slid open. "Oh come on, Corie. I'm counting on you to back me up."

"I can't in this case. Let me guarantee you, I'd want to have fair warning that someone was after me. If somebody has threatened this Katie recently, and she can finger him, perhaps the police could have him in custody in a matter of hours, before he has the chance to carry out any more mischief."

Alex stared at her for a moment before tossing her hands up in a helpless manner. "I swear, Corie, sometimes your imagination runs wilder than Val's."

"I did not imagine that my car window was shattered, nor did I imagine I was shot," Valerie pointed out.

"All right," Alex relented. "I can't fight the two of you. I'll check with the manager to see if there are any Katies in the building, but I won't do it tonight. I'll do it tomorrow."

"But Alex . . . "

"No buts." She pointed to the clock over the sink. "It's five after ten. I'm not disturbing the manager at this hour."

Valerie and Corinne exchanged wearied glances. Val would have felt better if they had started their own investigation immediately, but she was satisfied that Alex would help her. She needed the woman's cooperation in the matter and knew she'd find the intended victim more swiftly if Alex were on her side.

Though Alex kept the conversation upbeat before the two women retired for the night, when Val's head hit the pillow, her thoughts returned to the events of the early evening. She couldn't help it. Favoring her arm, she lay on her right side and thought about Katie. She had to reach her . . . she had to, before he did.

At some point, Val did drift off to sleep and the dreams

which played themselves out in her mind were terrifying ones. But they weren't of the shooting. They were the specific nightmares which had tormented her childhood . . . nightmares which had long ceased to haunt her—until that hour.

With the tragic scene from the pages of her past flaming in her memory, Valerie bolted up in bed. It hit her at once. There was no mistaken identity here. The past she had tried to push down and smother was suddenly looming before her again to destroy her future.

He was after Kaylene Valerie Quinn and he had found her!

Chapter 3

"**D**oes it hurt, Val?" Megan asked as she lightly touched the bandage through the sleeve.

The young woman tore her staring gaze from the pot of coffee before her and tried to rearrange an expression she knew was tense. "No, honey, it's not so bad."

"You're the most restless roomie I ever had. I was tempted to waken you a couple of times, then you quieted down. Bad dreams?" Alexandra asked pointedly.

Val nodded mutely, not wanting to think about them, and certainly not willing to discuss them. She reached for the pitcher of milk to pour over her banana and cornflakes.

"As soon as the breakfast dishes are done, Val, I'll take you to see the manager to find out if there are any Katies in the building."

Valerie's hand shook as she sat the pitcher down. Her anxious eyes lifted to Alex's and was relieved to see she didn't notice. Her attention was focused on her own cereal.

"I . . . I changed my mind," she stammered.

Now the older woman did look up. "You did? But you were so determined last night."

"Yes, last night I was. However, I've had time to think about it and I've come to the conclusion that your suggestion was the correct one; leave the investigation entirely up to the police."

"That's most sensible. Now, what about letting me do the story of your attack for the paper?" she asked, pressing her luck.

"No. I want this to be kept as quiet as possible. I won't do anything to embarrass Geoff."

"You? Embarrass Geoffrey?" she repeated with a note of amusement in her tone. "We're not talking scandal of the decade here. If a mind-your-own-business, quiet girl like you can become a victim, than any of us can. No . . . no . . . " she interrupted quickly when she saw Val's mouth open to protest. "I won't argue the point, although I will say, the incident would be reported but your name would be withheld."

Valerie couldn't contain her heavy sigh. Alex took another spoonful of cereal, then changed the subject. "Meg and I are going shopping today to look for that swimming suit you suggested. Want to come along and help me pick one out? I value your opinion."

"Thank you, but I have an appointment with one of my clients to coordinate drapery and slipcover material. That is, if she's willing to drive. Being without a car is going to be hard on business."

Alex reflected for a moment. "If you'd like to borrow mine . . . "

"No," Val cut in. "I refuse to put you out anymore than I already have."

"Stop talking nonsense. You're always welcome here,

Val, and if you want to spend another night, Megan and I would be glad to have you, wouldn't we, Meg?''

The little girl, now wearing a milk mustache, nodded in total agreement. ''You can even sleep in my room if you tell me a story.''

Valerie braved a smile of gratitude, thankful for her friends, but would they still be her friends if they really knew that she did have a scandal in her past? Val would rather let the man who shot her go free than ever have the nightmare she called her childhood be brought out in the open again. She could face almost anything but that.

As soon as the breakfast dishes were finished, Val excused herself to call Geoff. But she found herself staring at the phone a full minute before picking up the receiver, trying to gather the courage to make this difficult call. How could she tell him? She had never planned to tell him any of it.

Val dialed the office and it was picked up on the second ring. Corinne answered, but it took Geoffrey seemingly forever to come to the phone.

''Hello, Valerie. What's up?'' he greeted. There was a vague hint of impatience in his tone.

''You busy?''

''Extremely. I've got a few unexpected sick kids to work in between appointments this morning. I don't think they can wait until Monday. Something wrong?''

Now was not the time, she knew, to discuss something so personal . . . so distressing. Once again her own crisis would have to be put on hold. ''Will I see you this afternoon?''

''I'm afraid we'll have to shove that back until tonight. Right after work I plan to go down to Baltimore to pick up Mother for the holidays. Then I'll stop by your apartment

and bring you over to Stoneybrook around eight. I'm anxious for you two to finally meet.''

Valerie's heart sank. Not that she didn't want to meet
Monica Faraday, but it was imperative that she spend the
evening alone with Geoff. The atmosphere had to be or-
chestrated just right when she told him, which excluded any
third party, be it son or mother.

''Valerie? Are you still there?'' he queried when the line
became quiet.

''Yes. Do you love me, Geoff?''

''That goes without saying. Look, I'd really like to stand
here and chat but I'm pressed for time.''

In the background, Val could hear a child screaming.
''All right, Geoff. I'll see you tonight. Good-bye.''

When she placed the receiver back down, she looked up
to find a sober-looking Alex framed in the doorway. ''He's
got a waiting room full of children who need his attention,''
Val informed her. ''I couldn't tell him about the incident,
there simply wasn't time, but I will tell him tonight,'' she
promised. In her heart of hearts, though, she vowed that's
all she'd tell him.

Maybe knowing he had shot her would be punishment
enough. Maybe he would be satisfied to let it go at that.
Anyway, she had to hang on to that hope.

Valerie managed to pass a fairly normal morning, considering. She put last night's shooting from her mind as
best she could and lost herself in her work. She was successful up to a point, but *his* shadow was always crowding
around the edge of her memory. Val loved coordinating the
fabrics and wallpaper to beautify homes and it pleased her
deeply when her clients were well satisfied and referred her
to their friends. She understood their tastes and worked to
bring out the best for the least amount of money.

Once home, she did what she had intended to do the night before—soak in a bubble bath. Taking special care to keep her bandaged arm out of the bubbles, Val had been lingering for ten minutes when the phone rang. She counted the rings, knowing on the fifth her answering machine would kick in, so there was no need to hurry out of the tub and risk failing to answer it.

Valerie took her time, gave herself a pedicure, then, changing into a casual rose scoop-neck sweater and stretch denim leggings, she went out to the living room to return the call. It might be a prospective client. All she heard though, was a click. Some folks, she knew, did not like to speak to a machine, but if it was important, they would call back.

While Val was making a mug of hot chocolate, she decided to try a chicken quiche for supper. Alex had given her the recipe, a favorite of Geoff's, and since she wasn't going to see him till later, it seemed the perfect time to make it. Tossing a handful of miniature marshmallows into the beverage, Val returned to the living room and settled comfortably on the sofa. With the mug in one hand and a women's magazine on her lap, she began to idly browse through. Valerie especially enjoyed the layouts of homes, which she critiqued with a professional eye. Turning the pages, she came across an ad for a doll. A dreamy smile played on her lips. It was a very elegant Victorian bride doll. Her ivory gown had a lace overskirt and puffed leg o'mutton sleeves. She was a beauty, with a price tag to match.

Val took a slow sip, enjoying the lingering rich chocolaty flavor in her mouth. When she was a child, she and her father used to enjoy sipping mugs of cocoa in the evenings. The smile on her lips turned bittersweet at the memory. She never believed what they had said about him—never.

The phone at her elbow rang, interrupting her reverie. "Hello," she said pleasantly into the receiver. "Valerie Quinn speaking."

Silence.

Val hesitated, thinking the caller had reached a wrong number, but the receiver wasn't hastily replaced on the cradle. Unperturbed, she tried again. "Hello? Megan, honey, is that you?" Val took a slow sip and was about to replace the receiver herself when she became aware of a strange, crackling sound.

The young woman slid forward and quickly set the mug down on the coffee table; the magazine she'd been thumbing through tumbled face down on the carpet. Fire? Was she listening to the sound of a crackling fire?

"Who is this?" The question came out brusquely, knowing her caller had a sick sense of humor at the very least.

The receiver rang in her ear as the caller now slammed it down. Valerie placed hers back on its cradle. Yesterday, she would have dismissed this as a crank call, but not today. . . . Today it took on a chilly and macabre tone. Should she call Geoff? And if she did, what would she say? Valerie dismissed the idea almost at once. Besides, Geoffrey would be in Baltimore now.

The ringing of the phone sliced into her thoughts. She glanced warily at it and on the fourth ring, she picked it up.

"Hello," she all but snapped.

As she feared, there was no returned greeting. She listened with a sinking heart as she heard the click of a recorder being pressed on play. There were sounds of a vehicle driving, then she could hear the unmistakable strains of "Silent Night" playing in the background. Valerie drew her breath in quickly, knowing exactly what was coming.

" 'Hey, Katie,' " the voice said. Then she heard her

own voice played back. " 'No! Please don't!' " Following was the noise of a gunshot and the shattering of glass.

Though the line once again went dead, the scene played over and over in Valerie's mind like an old recording stuck in a groove. She sat rigid on the edge of the sofa, the receiver pressed to her pounding breast. Then it hit her as she placed it back on the cradle.

The man knew where she lived! This wasn't an isolated incident last night. And it was quite evident now, he was not going to let her alone.

Though Valerie had prepared herself to hear the phone ring a third time, when it did, she jumped, startled half out of her wits. She watched it with enormous eyes, determined not to answer this time . . . that if she ignored him, he'd surely get tired of his nerve-wearing games. Only he didn't.

Unable to stand it another second, she grabbed the receiver, fully expecting to hear that maddening recording again, but she heard a live voice this time.

"Katie? Katie, is that you?" the muffled voice queried.

Valerie swallowed hard before attempting to speak. That small, diminishing part of her which was still rational, cautioned, *Keep calm. Don't give this terrorist any further satisfaction.*

But try as she did, she couldn't disguise her fright. "Who is this? And why . . . why are you doing this to me?"

"Oh, Kaylene, you're a smart girl, you figure it out."

"Leave me alone! I'm not answering this phone anymore. Do you hear me? I'm not answering it!" And this time, she hung up on him.

"I have to get out of here," she said aloud, groping for a pair of loafers she knew she had shoved under the coffee table. She couldn't stay in that apartment alone any longer. A minute later she grabbed her coat and when she hastily let herself out the door, the phone had begun to ring again.

Her stalker watched her movements from within the phone booth. Valerie was running down the street—to her friend the cop, no doubt. Nervous fingers closed over the sizable pharmacy bag. "You think you're scared now, little girl, you just wait. This is only the beginning."

Ten minutes later, Valerie entered the police station slightly breathless and with mixed feelings. A part of her was hoping that Gil would be out, that one of the other officers would listen to her story. She would be more comfortable with a policewoman to verbalize her accusations, and her confessions, but this wasn't to be. Gil was sitting at the terminal, entering data in the computer when she came in. He glanced up, the beginning of a smile starting to form, then he caught himself. She looked terrible!

Rising, he assisted her to a chair across from his desk. "What's happened, Val?"

"He called me . . . again and again. I had to get away, I couldn't stay in that apartment a second longer."

"He?" He sat at the edge of the desk and looked at her. "You mean the man that shot you?"

Val nodded mutely as she slipped from her coat and eased it over the back of the chair. Her wide neckline dipped over her left shoulder, just barely exposing the top of her bandage, but she appeared too preoccupied to notice. "I want you to make him stop tormenting me."

Their eyes met and held. Gil chose his words carefully. "Yesterday, you were pretty sure the guy had mistaken you for somebody else. What made you change your mind?"

"Those calls," she reminded him. "He knows me."

"Do you know him, Val?"

She grimaced. "Yes."

He hesitated, waiting for her to continue. She looked so

frightened and vulnerable, and more like a teen in that casual outfit than the professional she was. ''Who is he?'' he prodded, knowing he had to deal with her gently.

Valerie whispered a name. He dipped his head to try to see the eyes that weren't quite willing to meet his now. ''Who?''

''Buddy Saget.''

''Buddy Saget,'' he repeated, but the name meant nothing to him. He tried again. ''Did he tell you his name?''

''He didn't have to. He knew me when we were children . . . when my name was Kaylene Valerie Quinn . . . Katie for short. I dropped the Kaylene after that . . . that dreadful night.''

Leaning forward, he cupped his palm under her chin and tilted her head so she would look at him. ''Val, listen to me. If you expect me to help you, you're going to have to explain exactly what this is all about.''

So in a rush of words, she told him. ''Twenty years ago this Christmas, Buddy Saget's mother, young cousin, and my father perished in a house fire. His aunt, while badly burned, said Daddy started it during an argument. And Buddy vowed that some day I'd have to pay for what Dad had done. I'd forgotten that promise; apparently Buddy hadn't.''

For a moment, Val thought the only thing she was aware of was the pounding of her heart and his stare. She saw not only surprise but disbelief on the face of this man who'd told her once that nothing he saw or heard shocked him anymore.

''Well, say something,'' she urged, breaking the nerve-wearing silence.

''Why in the name of common sense didn't you tell me about this before? If not back in high school, then last night, when I questioned you?''

"Because, I hadn't put the pieces of the puzzle together then. This happened so long ago that I'd managed to put that part of my life behind me. I had to, Gil, or it would have destroyed me," she admitted as she subconsciously twisted the strap of her shoulder bag.

As Gil watched those slender, restless fingers, he felt a wave of compassion sweep over him. "Can I get a cup of coffee for you? I find it's easier for people to talk if they can sip something."

"All right," Valerie consented. "I'd like cream."

"But no sugar, as I remember. You try to relax while I get it."

Relax? Val thought, with a vague morose smile. As she waited, she surveyed his desk top and was relieved to see he no longer had that old photograph of her in her cheerleader's uniform. It had been there, though, the day she'd stormed into the station and told him just what she thought of his airplane-pulling banner, declaring his love. She had finished by telling him to get rid of that ridiculous picture, then stalked out of the room, her head held high as the situation merited. She assumed he did get rid of it, especially now that she was engaged, but she never knew about Gil. His only predictability was the fact that he wasn't.

"You saved me a phone call," he said, breaking into her thoughts. "I was going to ask you to come on down and go through the mug books." Gil handed her the Styrofoam cup then, sprinkled a couple of cold medication tablets onto his palm, and swallowed them with his coffee.

Then Valerie remembered his own discomfort. "How are you feeling?"

"So-so. I've had better days," he admitted, opening a drawer to withdraw a small recorder. "Do you mind, Val?"

"Would it matter if I said yes?"

"I'll go along with your wishes, but I'm hoping you won't

protest. I don't always trust my memory when it comes to the fine details. I'm not going to pass it around for amusement, if that's in the back of your mind.''

She gave him a silent nod of approval. Pushing the record button, he leaned forward, his elbow propped on the uncluttered desk, his chin cupped in his palm. ''Tell me about the night your father set the fire.''

''He didn't set it, he was falsely accused,'' she said in defiant loyalty to a man who could not defend himself. Her eyes shifted from the recorder to Gil. ''My father had a landscaping business and he was doing some work over at the Saget farm. On the night of December twenty-sixth, Daddy had taken me for a ride, and on the way we stopped at the Saget's to discuss what kind of evergreens Mrs. Saget wanted planted in the front of the house. That was just an excuse to see her, because he wouldn't have planted them until spring. He and Ellen Saget were good friends.''

''How good?''

Even now she felt she was betraying her father to say it. ''Intimate. Of course I didn't know that at the time, it all came out later during the investigation. Before you judge my father, I want you to know he was a kind and loving parent to me.''

''I'm nobody's judge, Val. What about Mr. Saget?''

''He was killed a couple of years earlier when the tractor he was driving overturned on a hill and rolled on top of him.'' Val exhaled a deep sigh as she forced herself to talk about the night she'd blotted from her memory for so long. Now, it was difficult to separate fact from fantasy and she felt caught in a twilight of blended history and myth. ''Like most eventful days, it really started out quite ordinary, that was, until Ellen Saget's sister Eugenia arrived. Mrs. Saget had been caring for Eugenia's toddler while she was at work. She was angry with Daddy and they began to argue.''

"Ellen Saget?" he asked, not sure which of the two she meant.

"Eugenia. Daddy sent me out to the truck to wait for him, while Ellen sent her son to his room. Eugenia's little boy was asleep in the front bedroom. I remember wrapping myself in the blanket Daddy kept behind the seat. I must have fallen asleep, for my next memory was of suddenly waking up to hear screaming. When I looked out the windshield I saw the lower half of the house was engulfed in flames. The front door was locked from the inside, so I broke one of the panes with my bare hands. Just then, Buddy Saget came rushing out. He was wild, standing there in the snow in his bare feet and pajamas. Buddy screamed at me, saying that his aunt told him that Daddy started the fire. Then he tried to pull me inside the house, and he would have too, if it hadn't been for a neighbor man who arrived on the scene just then. He pulled me from his grasp and handed me over to his wife until help arrived."

Val took a quick sip of coffee to wet her dry mouth. "When he called today, he had played a tape which began with the sound of a crackling fire and ended with the actual taping of the gunshot he fired at me in the parking lot."

Gil stared at her for a long moment, scarcely able to take in her incredible story. "When that man called you Katie last night, why didn't that sound off an alarm up here?" he asked, tapping his temple.

"Because I haven't thought of myself as Katie for two decades now. When something terrible happens to you, you sometimes deal with it by not dealing with it. The tragedy broke both mother's health and spirit and she was never quite the same after that. Unwisely, she looked for solace in a bottle, which in the end only brought both of us more misery. That's why I never invited you to my place, Gil, and why I didn't want to get too close to your parents, especially your father. I sort of stood in awe of the man and I was afraid, if he found out about my family history, he'd reject me and he'd forbid us to date anymore.''

"No, Val, I know my father and he would never have done that. But had he known the problem, he would have tried to counsel you and perhaps even your mother if she would have let him.'' His hand closed over hers. "How I wish you would have trusted us enough to reach out for help.''

She drew back from his touch.

"You're still mistrustful, aren't you, Val?''

"I don't want your pity, Gilbert. I just want you to find this Saget person and arrest him.''

"All right,'' he said, becoming the professional again. "Let's go into the other room and look through the mug shots. Maybe we have some Sagets on file.''

Valerie picked up her cooling coffee and followed Gil into a small, windowless room, stuffy and poorly ventilated. After he placed the book in front of her, he pulled her sweater up over her shoulder. He couldn't help himself. Even now, in the midst of discussing something so serious, he found her shoulder so smooth and flawless—extremely distracting. If she was offended by his action, she didn't show it. Her mind was focused only on the pictures before her.

There were three Sagets on file . . . Aaron, Claire, and Gary. Val studied their faces, trying to connect anything familiar about these men to the hysterical boy who vowed to someday get her.

"Anything ring a bell?'' Gil asked with a hopeful note in his voice.

"Maybe. This fellow,'' she said, pointing to Gary, "has sandy hair like Buddy.''

"How old did you say this kid was at the time?''

"I didn't. About twelve, I think."

"That would make him roughly thirty-two now." He shook his head. "There might be a resemblance, but he's not going to look much like the character seared into your memory. Did you notice if he had any distinguishing features such as moles or scars, a prominent nose, crooked teeth?"

"No, but even if he had, such things can be cosmetically corrected. Oh, wait a minute," she interrupted herself. "His hands were burned that night, for he had tried putting out the fire before he grabbed me."

"If the burns were deep enough, he'd still have scars. I'll type the name into the computer and get a printout. CLEAN should be able to tell us something."

"Who?"

"CLEAN. It's an acronym for Commonwealth Law Enforcement Assistance Network. It's operated by the state police over in Harrisburg." He reflected for a moment before suggesting, "Maybe you could stay somewhere for a few days."

She closed the book and rose. "No. I won't leave town, Gil. I've got a business to run; I refuse to be driven away for who knows how long by some twisted fanatic. Just find him, so this nightmare can end."

"At least allow me to drive you home."

Valerie consented and went to gather her coat while Gil approached Conway, who'd just arrived, and spoke to him in a low tone. Gil's words yesterday now almost seemed prophetic. *If you needed my professional help, I'd give it to you.* And here she was, almost begging after she'd refused him her services.

Down deep inside she knew that Gil was truly concerned and not trying to be manipulative in any way. Her conscience pricked her. She was engaged to a handsome pediatrician with a promising future, but a part of her was still drawn to the flaxen-haired cop who had not only been her football hero, but her first and only love during her lonely teen years.

Val's small two-story brick apartment was situated atop her rented studio. She wasn't surprised that Gil didn't just drop her off, but entered the building with her to check it out. He followed her up the narrow staircase to her domicile. Wordlessly, she unlocked the door to her living room and he stepped inside.

The phone began to ring. Valerie visibly jumped, her nerves raw, and turned to Gil. He nodded and trailed right behind her, taking a place at her side so he could hear. Her "hello" was scarcely a whisper.

"Valerie? Is that you?"

The young woman sank down on the sofa, her knees weak with relief. "Oh Geoffrey, it's so good to hear your voice."

"Where have you been? I tried to get you several times but all I got was that answering machine."

"I was out." Her anxious eyes flickered to meet Gil's. "I just got in the door when the phone started ringing."

"Rushing around as usual. No wonder you sound winded. Listen, Val, I'm afraid I won't be able to make it tonight."

Don't say that! I need you! her mind screamed, but the words which came out of her mouth were surprisingly calm. "Why not, Geoff? I was counting on us spending time alone tonight."

"Don't make me feel any worse than I already do, woman," he said with a chuckle, not understanding that a soul-bearing talk, and not romance, was on her mind. "Mother Nature pulled a fast one. I'm in Baltimore, standing here looking out the window at a freezing rain. The traffic's barely moving. Mother convinced me it's suicide to try and drive in this, so we'll head back tomorrow. I know you're disappointed, but I'll make it up to you. I think we just might have cause to celebrate.''

"Why?"

"I prefer to tell you in person. I'll see you around noon." Then he added with a chuckle, "I hope. Good night, Val."

"Good night, Geoffrey." Then she replaced the receiver on its cradle. "That man's never around when I need him!" she complained, then bit her lip. The very last thing she wanted to do in front of Gil was to put Geoff in an unfavorable light. "There's a freezing rain falling over Baltimore. He isn't returning tonight," she said needlessly.

He picked the receiver right back up and handed it to her. "Call Alexandra. Ask her if it's all right if you spend the night with her."

Too weary to argue, she dialed the woman's number. There was no answer. Gil asked her to check her incoming calls. He said maybe Saget, or whoever it was that was harassing her, would have left a message. Val doubted it, but mutely did as she was told. There was a call from a client who said she couldn't keep their Monday morning appointment, but none from her tormentor. Setting the phone aside, she braved a smile.

"I'll try Alex again in a half hour. Meanwhile, I suppose you'd better be getting back to the station."

Was there something in the tenor of her voice which said *But I wish you wouldn't*, Gil wondered as he sat down beside her. "Actually, I'm off duty until Monday morning, but I won't be off duty from this case. It'll be with me, twenty-four hours a day."

That brave smile turned shy. "I'm glad you're on this one. I remember what a fighter and go-getter you were out on the field."

"And you know why? I had my favorite cheerleader in there, urging me to victory. We're going to win this one too, Val. That character may not know it yet, but he's bitten off more than he can chew. When he targeted you, he took on me as well."

Val felt hot tears threatening her eyes. "Oh Gil, I wish . . ."

"What do you wish?" he prodded when she broke off so abruptly.

She looked at him now, his face so close to hers. *I wish we would never have gone our separate ways*, she wanted to say, but couldn't. A man like Gil needed little encouragement and she knew, as vulnerable as she was, it wouldn't take much to climb into his arms and feel absolutely horrible about it afterward. Her future was with Geoffrey, and she was determined to remain true to her commitment. If only he were here. Saget knew where she lived, he knew where he could find her. She bit her lip to keep from crying and at that moment, she was aware of Gil's fingers pulling her slipping garment back over her shoulder.

"Does that bother you?"

"You'd better believe it does!"

She smiled in spite of herself. "It's the style and it's suppose to drape."

"In that case, it can't be very comfortable for you, and I know sure as I'm sitting here, it isn't for me. It's downright titillating. Talk about a sly means of torment!"

They both laughed and with that laughter came a feeling of release for Val. She smiled, then changed the subject and asked him what made him choose law enforcement as his vocation.

He reflected a moment, his eyes leaving her face to fasten on the blank TV screen. "I guess the truth of the matter is, I stumbled into it. Dad would have been thrilled had I followed in his footsteps, but he never pushed me in that direction. He said I must follow my natural bent, and whatever it was, I should be the best in my chosen field. He said never to compromise myself, and never lose my integrity, even if all those around me were. It was great advice, offered from a man who followed it himself.

"I always wanted a job where I could serve people. I was a volunteer fireman for awhile . . . drove an ambulance too. I got to know a lot of the people involved in emergency work. I admired them—they were my heroes. I enrolled in some courses in criminal justice and worked toward a degree, then joined the Philadelphia police department and moved up in rank rather quickly. I was a plainclothes detective there." His gaze left the screen now to settle on her. "I did my share of undercover work too. It's interesting but dangerous work. Every two and a half days, a policeman loses his life in the line of duty. I can't ever allow myself to become careless, because if I do, I become even more vulnerable."

Valerie listened to him, forgetting for a little while, at least, her own fears and the lingering horror of the past twenty-four hours. It occurred to her for the first time that she was drawn to men who were the protectors of life— Geoffrey in the medical field, and Gil in law enforcement.

"You must feel a sense of pride when the job goes well and the criminal's safe behind bars."

"Trouble is, he doesn't always stay there. I've seen drug dealers whom we've risked our lives to get off the streets be released because of a technicality. Then there's the matter of an unsympathetic press. Granted, sometimes it's deserved, but remember, there's bad apples in every profession which ought to be weeded out, but aren't until there's a public outcry."

He clasped his hands before him and leaned forward, his

elbows on his knees as he continued to speak from his heart. "The fabric of our society is coming apart, Val. I see the main cause as the breakup of the family. There's no father figure, especially in the urban areas, for the kids to look up to anymore. And mother's struggling to put food on the table and a roof over their heads, so she can't be involved in their lives as the average woman was thirty years ago. Dad used to say, 'The best thing I can do for you kids is to love your mother.' I didn't realize until I was older what he meant or how lucky I was growing up in an intact family who really cared about each other. I didn't always see it that way, though. I was the only son, born smack dab in the middle of four sisters, whom I viewed as super pains-in-the-neck."

Valerie actually found herself laughing. "Oh yes, I do remember one of the girls running to your mother every time I was over at your place, complaining about what you did to them. I can't be entirely sympathetic to your plight, Gilbert. You were a born tease and a precocious kid if ever there was one."

"And I suppose some of that has spilled over into my adulthood, right?" There was a twinkle in her eye which hadn't been there before. Her smile gave him confidence. "What do you say, you and I go out for something to eat."

That smile slowly vanished. "I don't know if that's a good idea."

"Why not? It's supper time and seeing neither of us have any plans for the evening, I think it would be nice if we eat together. If it makes you feel better, don't approach this as a date. And as far as Geoffrey's concerned, I'm sure he'd appreciate the fact a man was looking out for you in his absence—a cop, no less."

"Well," she hedged, "since you put it that way, okay. Give me a few minutes to change into something less . . .

tormenting for you,'' she said with a chuckle, choosing his own words.

He watched her get up and exit before turning his attention back to the room he found himself in. Though the furnishings weren't pretentious, they were attractive and serviceable. The sofa and the curtains were of the same subdued red and gray pattern. The two built-in cabinets were painted a dazzling white, as was the rocker. The basket table before him held a blood-red poinsettia, a ceramic Santa, and a *Country Homes* magazine. Rising, he walked over to one of the cabinets, which comprised four shelves. They displayed the usual arrangements of knick-knacks and photographs. There was a small stuffed bear on the bottom shelf, a replica of their school mascot. He'd bought it for her during their senior year. Imagine, her keeping that after all these years. A smile played on his lips as he looked over the array of photographs. One in particular caught his interest. It was of a burly red head in a brown suit. Holding his hand was a small girl in pigtails and a plaid dress. Had only Quinn realized the heartbreak his action would cause his only child before he did it.

Gil moved on to another photograph. This was of Valerie also—very beautiful, very recent, and very engaged to the tall, handsome man at her side. *Don't be too sure of yourself, Faraday. You haven't gotten Val to the altar yet, and if I have my way . . .*

The rest of his thoughts were shattered at that point. Turning, he rushed to the source of Valerie's hysterical screaming, not knowing what to expect, but ready for anything.

Chapter 4

Valerie applied blush to her cheeks, thinking she still looked a bit pale, then reached for an atomizer, but paused, her hand midway.

No. This was not a date. This was simply sharing a dinner with an old acquaintance. She surveyed her sweater, which kept sliding off her shoulder, and knew she'd better change into something less distracting. Val certainly didn't want to give Gilbert any encouragement by adorning herself provocatively. There was a blue, long-sleeved corduroy dress she'd bought recently but hadn't worn yet which would do nicely. It was the epitome of primness. She went directly to her closet and opened the door. As she took a step inside, she trod on something soft and bent over to pick it up.

Valerie didn't see it clearly until she stepped back from the shadows, and even then she couldn't believe what her brain told her she was holding. And her reaction couldn't have been any quicker had it been a live serpent in her grasp. Tossing it into the air, it landed, of all places, face up on her bed.

Her stomach reacted violently and after letting out a loud scream, she raced back into the bathroom. Dropping to her knees, she hung over the bowl and gagged.

Gil rounded the corner and paused. He'd expected many things, but this was not one of them. Hesitating only an instant, he joined her and placed a consoling hand across her back. "Val, what is it? What's happened to you?"

When she lifted her face, there were tears running down her cheeks. "He not only knows where I live, now he's been here. Gil, he was here!"

He looked at her hard. "What?"

"Over there . . . on the bed, he left his calling card," she said, pointing a shaky finger into the other room.

She watched as he went out for the object, and when he returned, he had it in his hand and a puzzled expression on his brow.

Valerie jumped back against the tile wall. "Keep that thing away from me!"

He looked down at the burned doll. "I have a pretty good idea what it means, but perhaps you'd better tell me, as I'm sure you do know."

The young woman nodded. "The doll was a Christmas present from Daddy, but when I went out to the truck to wait for him, I forgot to take it along. It . . . it burned up in the house," she finished with a choking sob.

Laying the charred toy aside, he wrapped his arms around her. She didn't pull away; her response was to cling to him as he consolingly stroked her back. Gilbert said nothing, but the question kept echoing in his mind. Just what kind of a warped and twisted mind were they dealing with here?

As he stood there in deep thought, his arms still enveloping her, he became aware that her sobbing had ceased and she was now staring up at him expectantly. "What do we do now?" she asked in a small voice when their eyes met and held.

"What I intended to do, take you out to eat."

She drew back; where was this man's sensitivity? "Now? Gil, you can't possibly expect me to go out among people tonight. My nerves are shot."

"You're probably right. Pack an overnight case. We'll stop and get a pizza on the way to my place."

"Your place? I can't do that; I'm engaged."

Yeah, to the wrong guy, he thought, then spoke in an authoritative voice she seldom heard. "Val, either you spend the night at my place or I spend it here. You're not going to stay alone and that's not open for discussion."

As Val accompanied him to the hardware store to choose a new lock for her door, she didn't know whether she was more annoyed with his I'm-in-charge-and-you're-going-to-listen attitude, or more grateful, but she supposed it was the latter. It was hard to think rationally when she was scared half out of her wits.

A half hour later, Valerie's eyes swept up the rambling, Victorian house, complete with turrents and gingerbread trim. In the darkness, one couldn't see the peeling gray paint, or the sagging side porch. It had gone on the market remarkably cheap as a handyman's special, and Valerie still deeply resented the fact that Gil had outbid her for something she knew darn well he didn't really want. She had seen the possibility for a lovely studio in the large room containing the front bay window—certainly a far better location than her side street apartment. And what she was paying in rent for the shop and her apartment would have been no more than she would be paying in mortgage. And one day, it would have been all hers—perhaps sooner than she had planned if her business continued to grow as it was. But now? . . . She heaved a weary sigh and fell into step as they walked side by side down the cracked cement walk and up on the front porch. After inserting the key, he turned to her.

"Welcome to Victorian Rose."

She blinked up at him, not able to see his features clearly in the darkness. "What?"

"Victorian Rose," he repeated. "If the baby doctor can name his house, I suppose I can too."

She was about to tell him his constant reference to Geoffrey by that disparaging term was distasteful to her, but her thoughts were interrupted by the menacing deep barks of a canine. She jumped back. "Good heavens, what have you got locked up in there?"

"Brutus. He won't hurt you as long as he senses you're a friend of mine." He winked. "So behave yourself, kiddo."

Gil unlocked the door and flipped on the light before giving his pet a playful rub along his handsome gray coat. He turned to Val, who was standing by the door, ready for a hasty exit if she were the least bit threatened by this intimidating-looking beast.

Amusement touched Gil's face. "Come on in, Val. He won't attack unless I give the command. Honest."

She stepped farther inside, then hesitantly joined the pair.

"Brutus," he said, turning to face the German shepherd, "this is Valerie, an old friend of mine." Then to her, "Val, this is Brutus, my former partner."

"Partner?" she asked with a skeptical lift of her brow.

"Yeah," he grinned. "We worked together on several cases, but now the poor boy's developed arthritis in his hips from too much sitting in patrol cars. When he was retired from the force, I took him as a pet, but he misses the action of catching all those bad guys, don't you, Brute?"

Brute barked. Val didn't know whether to jump back or laugh; she did the latter.

"He senses your nervousness. Pat his head, let him get your scent."

The young decorator hesitantly did as Gil suggested.

"Good. Now relax in the living room while I reheat the pizza and pour some soda for us. Brute will keep you company."

Valerie opened her mouth to insist she didn't really need or want the companionship of a police dog, but Gil was out of the room before she could voice her opinion. Her eyes shifted suspiciously to the dog, who was watching her.

"Nice doggie," she whispered, clearly not trusting him. A part of her was afraid that when she turned her back, he would be on her as though she were a criminal, yet the more rational part told her she was being silly. If he were dangerous, Gil wouldn't leave him alone with her. Squaring her shoulders, she turned and entered the large room she had once had designs on for her studio.

A live Christmas tree occupying the far corner drew Val like a magnet. Gil had decorated it with a mix-match of old and new ornaments. One leaped out at her and she couldn't resist the temptation to turn the shiny brass angel-shaped figure around to read the inscription on the back.

TO GIL
ALL MY LOVE
VAL 12/25/83

She remembered the cold winter day she had stood outside the jewelry store and seen it in the window. He'd called her his angel the night before, and now on impulse she had rushed inside and bought the ornament with money saved by baby sitting. Val recalled that when he'd opened it, she had said it was the first item she had purchased for their life together. Had she actually been that bold? That presumptuous? They were only seventeen—kids—but she loved him with all her heart, or so she thought at the time.

Valerie heard a step behind her and turned. Gil was just setting a tray on the magazine-cluttered coffee table.

"You've kept it all these years," she commented, letting the ornament fall back into place.

"Why not?" He smiled, exposing that single dimple Val used to find so appealing and it bothered her now to find that she still did. "I noticed you've saved that little stuffed teddy bear too."

"I never was one to throw out gifts from friends," she excused herself lamely.

"Me neither," he said, his eyes meeting hers, then he went on. "Have a seat while I get the fire going and . . . " He broke off as he noticed Brutus edging toward the pizza. "Don't you even think about it, pal. When I eat, you'll eat."

Val was surprised to see that the dog obeyed, stretching out on the rug, his chin resting on his paws. Gil went on, "I have three fireplaces here, but this is the only one in working condition. Little by little, though, I'll get things fixed up and Victorian Rose will be the most eye-catching house on the block. This summer I intend to give her a fresh coat of gray paint . . . "

"Gray?" Val couldn't help but cut in. "It would be so much more esthetic if it were a pale yellow with white trim."

He considered this a moment as he wiped his lightly soiled hands on his hips. "You might have a point there. Let's eat," he said, sitting down beside her.

She handed him a wedge, which he promptly gave to the dog. "There you go, Brute."

"Must you keep calling him that?"

"Don't trust him yet, huh? A guy could feel insulted."

"But you don't. You're grinning."

He accepted the slice she passed to him and changed the subject. "Next month, I intend to start working on this room. I'd like wall-to-wall carpeting and . . ."

"No . . . !"

He glanced up innocently. "Excuse me?"

"No. No wall-to-wall. Gil, this is a Victorian home, so keep with that theme. I'd choose a lovely oriental rug. The walls appear in great shape, so you could paint or paper. And as far as furniture goes, we have a lovely antique shop at the intersection which carries furnishings just made for this place and . . ." She broke off, suddenly aware that he was watching her with quiet amusement. "Gilbert Ellis! Shame on you, telling me things you have no intention of doing just to get me interested in decorating your house for you. I'm not interested."

"Oh yes you are! You love a challenge." He bit into his pizza. "And so do I."

Valerie reached for her soda, pretending she hadn't heard that last comment.

They ate the rest of their light supper in silence. Val was surprised she could eat at all. Her nervous stomach had calmed down and the earlier event now seemed like a bad dream. Gil turned the tree lights on and the table light out, and with the flickering glow of the fire, the room took on a romantic atmosphere. She was afraid he was going to take advantage of the moment—he would have back in the old days. But now he seemed perfectly content to just sit beside her on the sofa, his arms folded and his dog sitting at his feet.

The overall atmosphere had a calming effect on Val, and as the night wore on, she grew more and more at ease with this man who asked nothing of her other than to share her company. He'd changed into jeans and a navy pullover, making it easier for her to forget he was a cop. She slipped out of her pumps and drew her feet up under her long skirt and began to talk about her past as she never had to anyone before. Gil listened without comment, fascinated, yet saddened that she'd felt the need to keep all this bottled inside for so many years. She spoke of her desire to surround herself with pretty, though not necessarily expensive things to counterbalance the ugly part of her childhood. She told him of her modest doll collection and how thrilled she was that a store specializing in the sale of both new and old dolls had recently opened up in town. She was setting a few dollars aside each week in her tight budget to purchase one— probably a storybook character doll if they carried anything in that line. She also confessed that her appreciation for beauty and her artistic eye had drawn her into the field of interior decorating, although her earliest desire was to be a nurse. She wanted to help hurting children as nurses had helped her.

"About a year after the fire, we moved into town and I decided that along with a new residence and a new school, I'd have a new name as well. I began using my middle name, Valerie. My other name, Kaylene, was a contraction of mother's name, Kay Marlene. But I preferred Valerie, I always have. It means, 'to be strong.' " She smiled ruefully. "It was a challenge living up to it, believe me. All through my school years I wanted so badly to belong . . . to be accepted and blend in with everyone else. That's why I sang in the chorus and became a cheerleader. Outwardly, I suppose I was somewhat successful, but inside, oh my, that was a different story entirely. I lived in constant fear that someone would find out about my family history and I'd become the scandal of Cedarcrest High. I thought my past was behind me and now . . . " Her voice broke. "Now it seems to have caught up once again, and Gil, it's so much worse than I ever imagined.''

His emotions stirred, Gilbert reached for her hand and brought it to his lips before Val realized what he was doing.

''No, don't!'' she cried out, and drew her fingers out of his clasp, never feeling more conscious of those old scars than at that moment. Valerie got up from the sofa and walked over to the hearth. And with her back to him, she told him she didn't want his pity.

Though Gil joined her he hesitated a moment before placing his hand upon her shoulder. ''I don't pity you, Val, but I do think it's a pity you feel it necessary to shut yourself off from those who can comfort you.'' He turned her around and made her face him. ''I've listened to you, now it's only fair you listen to me. You've weathered the storms of living in the turbulence of a dysfunctional family to emerge a better person. You don't want to wallow in self-pity or follow in your mother's footsteps and I admire you for it. Val, I've seen kids who've had every advantage possible, only to toss their future and sometimes their very lives away because they were foolish enough to get hooked on booze or drugs. On the other hand, I've seen kids raised by abusive, uncaring parents grow up determined to break the chains of bondage with their past and become productive members of society. I can't figure it, but I suppose it pretty much boils down to choice. Good or bad, we choose the paths we follow. So stop beating up on yourself for something you had no control over. Stop allowing the past to dictate your future.''

She smiled up at him, feeling deeply grateful for his understanding and nonjudgmental attitude. Had she only confided in him years ago. Though she couldn't turn back the clock, she could open her heart a bit more now. ''I think I lived most of my childhood in a dream world where I was safe and nothing could touch me. I must have read every fairy tale ever written.''

"And you were always the princess."

She nodded. "One day, when I was quite young, I even caught a frog thinking that if I could . . . '' She broke off, realizing how totally off the wall and foolish she must be sounding. Val bit her lip, expecting him to laugh any second. Only he didn't.

Instead, he dipped his head so he could look into her embarrassed eyes and said in a voice so serious it made her mouth slide open, "Your prince has come, angel, though he hasn't come riding in on a white horse. You haven't recognized him yet, but you will. You will."

She watched him, knowing what was on his mind. His eyes after all, were focused on her lips. His mouth met hers in a succession of soft kisses that sent her heart racing. This was wrong! There was Geoffrey to consider. What would he think? And suddenly she felt every bit as guilty as she imagined her father must have, or should have felt when he was stealing those secret moments with the Saget woman. Still, it took every bit of willpower she could muster to ease herself from his embrace. She expected him to retort, but the protest came from deep within Brutus's throat as he uttered a low growl.

Startled, Val looked over at him. He was watching her, his body tense, ready for a command from his master.

Gil spoke a few words to him, then the dog sat back down and stretched out. "He's very protective of me. I tend to forget that sometimes."

Valerie ran a wearied hand through her hair. "Gil, I really shouldn't be here."

"Oh? And where should you be?"

She shook her head, tears welling in her eyes. "Maybe I should call Alex. Surely she's home by now."

"Val, it's nearly one A.M."

"It is?" She was amazed at how quickly the time was ticking by. "Oh, Gilbert, I'm becoming afraid again."

"I won't let him hurt you. That's why you're here."

"At this point, I'm not sure if I'm more afraid of him or myself," she confessed. "I'm engaged, and don't you dare say 'to the wrong man,' or so help me, I'll scream."

"No need for me to remind you of something you already know." He went over to the foyer to retrieve her overnight bag, then informed her, "The only bedroom furnished is mine, so I hope you don't mind a roomie."

"Gil Ellis, you're a . . . "

"Brute," he interrupted as a smile slipped across his face. "I'm referring to Brute, so put your suspicious little mind to rest. He likes to curl up on his favorite rag rug at the foot of my bed. No reason he should be barred from my room just because I am. It'll give you an opportunity to get to know each other. I'd like you two to be friends."

That took some stretch of the imagination, Val thought, but said, "I hope if I have to use the bathroom during the night, he'll let me."

"Just ask him nicely," he said with a grin.

And that grin softened Val; she could never stay angry at him for very long. "Where will you sleep?"

He pointed to the lumpy mauve sofa they had been sitting on a short while ago. "Don't worry about me. I've slept in a lot more uncomfortable places before."

That was the least of Val's worries, she thought as she trailed him up the stairs. She was concerned about how on earth she'd ever explain to her fiancé, were he to find out that she had spent the night at the home of her old boyfriend. And knowing Geoffrey as she did, he'd suspect the worst.

Chapter 5

Caught in the grip of unsettling dreams, Valerie moved restlessly beneath the heavy quilt. It was to be her shining hour, standing with Geoffrey at the altar in front of all his friends. The preacher looked out over the wedding guests.

"If there's any reason why this man and this woman cannot be lawfully joined together, speak now or forever hold your peace."

Val watched in horror as a young boy in pajamas rose up in the middle of the congregation and pointed an accusing finger at her. "She cannot be allowed to marry Dr. Faraday, because Kaylene's the daughter of the man that killed my family when he set our house on fire!"

The young woman gasped and bolted up in bed. It was a dream, only a dream, she assured herself, raking her hair back off her face. Darting eyes still wild with fright, she immediately became aware of her surroundings. She wasn't in a church, nor was she at home, but in Gil's shiny brass bed. The furnishings were sparse, consisting of a home gym in one corner and a large pine dresser along the wall. Her overnight bag stood next to an old straight-back chair where she'd neatly laid her dress before retiring. A night stand completed the picture.

The sun was up and the door was standing ajar. She looked warily about for Brutus now, but didn't see him. Gil must have opened it to let him out; she distinctly remembered latching it last night. Her eyes swept down over her flannel nightshirt; she didn't like the thought of him possibly gawking at her when she was sound asleep. Considering the past thirty-six hours, she'd enjoyed a sound sleep once she finally dozed off. Brutus had given her one puzzled what-are-you-doing-sleeping-in-my-master's bed kind of look before curling up on the rag rug and closing his eyes. Then neither bothered the other for the rest of the night.

Valerie took a quick bath in the quaint claw leg tub before changing into fresh lingerie and last night's dress. This room, like some of the others in the vintage house, intrigued her and sparked her imagination. Once a bedroom, but now a bathroom, it still needed a lot of renovation, although one thing she hoped Gil wouldn't change was the fireplace. She could envision many cozy possibilities here.

Aromas of frying eggs and potatoes drew her into the old-fashioned kitchen, where she found Gil busy preparing breakfast. His back to her, he was attired in faded blue jeans and undershirt, and his feet were covered only with a pair of white tube socks. Brutus, forever the observant one, announced her presence with a single bark.

Now Gilbert looked over his shoulder and grinned, waving the turner he was holding by way of greeting. "Good morning, Val. Have a seat. Everything's just about ready."

Valerie glanced at the place settings on the oval table. One had a mug with the words SUPER COP engraved on it. Pulling out the captain's chair at the other setting, she sat down. "You should have called me, Gil. I would have gladly helped."

He carried the large skillet over to her and lifted a generous portion of potatoes and scrambled eggs on her plate. "I know, and I was tempted, but then I figured you probably didn't have much sleep lately, so I let you rest until you naturally awakened." He then reached for the rye toast that had just popped up, handed her a piece, and sat down. There was an insulated pot of coffee on the center of the table beside an aluminum plate of shoofly pie. Its label, bearing the name of a local farmer's market, was visible through the plastic. She took a sip of freshly squeezed orange juice, impressed with the layout.

They ate in silence for a few moments. "Where did you ever learn to cook like this?"

"I grew tired of eating in restaurants, so with Mom's guidance via the telephone, I learned. The first few tries were disastrous, though. I either burned or overcooked everything I tried, but now I think I've mastered it to suit my tastes. I make some pretty good potato filling and chicken corn pie, if I must say so myself. Of course, with the house needing so much repair, I won't have time to hone my culinary skills further."

"It's all quite delicious."

"Thanks. You digging in like you are is the best compliment you can give me." He bit into his crunchy toast before continuing. "My sister Jenny's coming over with her three kids for Christmas dinner. Her husband's off in the military, so I thought her boys needed a male figure. I've stepped in to help out when I can. They love to come over here and romp around with Brutus. They're good kids."

As Valerie watched him dig into those green pepper and

onion flavored home fries, her heart softened. She found this unexpected domestic bent in his personality appealing. Val felt very comfortable with him . . . comfortable enough to ask a question which had entered her mind before.

"Did you ever find someone you'd thought you'd like to settle down with?"

He lifted a quizzical brow. "You mean besides you? Yes, as a matter of fact, I did. Two years ago I almost walked down the aisle with a girl named Pamela. She was twenty-two, rich, had the prettiest face and the most fantastic figure you could imagine. I mean, she was world-class—every man's dream."

Valerie bristled. "I might have expected that kind of a response from you. There's more to a woman than her face and body, Gilbert Ellis."

"You jealous?" he asked with a twinkling tease in his eye.

"Certainly not!"

"You could have fooled me."

Val sighed, wondering why she was even having this conversation with a man who stirred up such a potpourri of emotions inside her. "Wipe that silly grin off your face. I suppose you won't be satisfied until I ask you what happened."

"Oh, I think it's the other way around, Quinn. You're just dying of curiosity."

"She dumped you, didn't she, for a wealthier, more elite type of guy. Smart girl."

"It wasn't quite like that." His smile faded as he thought back over it. "I'd better go back to how we met in the first place. I was working undercover on a drug detail. While I was waiting for my contact, I saw this young woman attacked. I took the assailant on and wrestled the knife from him. But trying to get the lady to realize I was on her side was another matter. She was hysterical and the bearded, mangy character standing before her in scuffy clothes was not exactly how she pictured Philadelphia's finest. He cut a wedge of the shoofly pie. "Anyway, I wanted her to have the proper opinion of me, and so the next night I called to see how she was doing. We talked awhile and I invited her out to dinner. She accepted and it was the beginning of a whirlwind courtship. I enjoyed her appreciation of me, and she confused gratitude with love. We came from such diverse backgrounds. She was from a wealthy old Philadelphia family. The attraction was purely physical, and luckily we realized that before we made a bad mistake." He took a bite of the gooey-bottomed cake and studied the woman across the table from him for a moment.

"I think, Val, you're as confused now as we were back then. I just hope you come to your senses in time, before you make the mistake of your life. You're very vulnerable, so don't lean too heavily on your feelings. They can't be trusted. Faraday makes sick kids better. You remember a time in your own life when you looked up to the doctors and nurses who took care of you. You told me so yourself, remember. Pam fed my ego, blinded my own common sense, but when we came right down to it, we had precious little in common. Certainly not enough to build a marriage on."

He waited for her to say something, but when she didn't, he continued. "You're going to have to tell Faraday everything about Saget, and I do mean everything, Val. If you're so bent on marrying this guy, don't begin your marriage with secrets."

"I'll tell him about Saget," she said as she carried her empty plate over to the sink. *But not quite everything*, she silently vowed. Geoffrey came from a wealthy family; she from a working class one, her own father accused of arson and the deaths of three people. How on earth could she ever expect Geoffrey to accept that?

An hour later, the couple were back at Valerie's apartment. She stood by, watching as Gil added the new lock on her door. "You know," he commented as he worked, "you had the worst possible lock. This one could have been opened with everything from a credit card to a pipe wrench, and even more quickly than with a key. What I'm putting on here is the best choice, a deadbolt lock. It must be locked or unlocked with a key from either side."

"Why do they call it a deadbolt?"

"Because the long bolt which locks into the door frame isn't spring loaded and is immovable unless the frame is dismantled. That would take tremendous force, a great deal of noise, and a lot of time. Here," he said, handing her a key. "Unlock it."

"Why do you have it so high?"

"To install it properly, it should be at your eye level. This makes it five times more difficult for someone to force open the door than if the lock were waist high. It should make you feel more secure, but if it's still not enough to give you peace of mind I can loan you Brutus."

"Don't be ridiculous. Brutus doesn't like me."

"If you want to win his friendship, you've got to be friendly to him, just like with people, Val."

She shot him a look of annoyance, then unlocked the door and opened it. Her lips parted and she inwardly groaned, watching the tall, handsome physician enter below and climb the narrow, carpeted staircase. Eyes sweeping up to fix on hers, his lips drew back immediately and he walked right in. Not noticing Gil, he greeted her with a heartfelt hug which she didn't enthusiastically return. Then, sensing they weren't alone, he turned to face the man behind him.

"Oh. Good morning," he said curtly.

"Doc," Gil replied with a slight nod of recognition.

Valerie forced a smile, feeling she had to say something. "Geoffrey, you remember Lt. Ellis."

"Of course. How could I ever forget the guy who hired the banner-flying plane?"

The young woman sighed, feeling the tension accelerate. She had hoped to have Gil out by the time Geoffrey arrived. But the installation took longer and Geoff came sooner than expected. "The lieutenant was just installing a new lock system for me," she said, feeling the need to explain her former boyfriend's presence.

"What's wrong with the one you had?" he asked innocently.

"It's not burglar-proof, that's what," Gil said, placing his tools back into his metal chest. "Last night someone entered, using a credit card is my guess."

Geoffrey frowned, unconsciously adjusting his wire frame glasses, and glanced about. The room didn't look disturbed. "What did he take?"

"Only my sense of security and peace of mind," said Val.

"I don't understand. Someone breaks in but doesn't steal anything?" His arm slid around Valerie's shoulder and his hand came to rest on her bandaged arm. That frown cut deeper into his brow. "What's this?"

"It's nothing to be concerned about, Geoff."

"Val," Gil spoke, impatience cutting into his tone. "Tell him."

Valerie looked from one man to the other. Both were staring at her—one with a look of urgency, and the other quizzically. There was no easy way to break it to him. "I was . . . shot Friday evening."

That puzzled look was replaced by one of stark disbelief. "You were what! My gosh, Val . . . "

Raising a silencing hand, she quickly tried to reassure him. "I'm okay, really. It's just a flesh wound which Doctor Cantrell treated in the E.R. I'm scarcely conscious of it unless I bump it."

He looked at Gil once again. "Who did this? Do you know?"

"We have a pretty good idea."

"In that case, don't you think the sensible thing to do is to go out and make an arrest?"

"I can't just yet. At present we have three possible suspects, and they're being checked into now. As soon as we're positive we've targeted the right guy, we'll move in and make that arrest." Gil hesitated before adding, "He's also been harassing her by phone. She probably should get an unlisted number, if it weren't such a problem for her business."

Geoffrey turned to Valerie now, unable to comprehend that something like this could happen. "Why didn't you tell me about this? I spoke to you both Saturday morning and evening."

"I tried to, Geoffrey, but you were so busy at the office. Then when we spoke later, I just figured it would be better if I told you in person. I was afraid you would have tried to drive home over icy roads had you known."

Gil settled in the rocker, stretched his long legs out in front, and folded his arms across his chest. Geoffrey turned, distracted by the creaking runners. Resentment at this man who seemed so familiar in Valerie's home rippled through him. He was affronted by Gil's carefree dress style and the biceps so visible beneath his tee shirt, and by his doing projects for Valerie that Geoff should be doing. "How long will it be until you make an arrest?" he asked, tight-lipped.

"I already told you. Whenever we've sure we have the right guy."

"That's no answer. What are we talking about here, a day? A week? How long? You must have some idea."

"A ballpark figure—forty-eight hours. I want to move cautiously. I don't want him hiring some fast-talking lawyer who will find a way to throw the case out because of some loophole in the system or because I didn't follow procedures."

Geoffrey was thoughtful a moment. "Valerie's an attractive young woman and she's easy prey for some sick mind. For all we know, it could even be one of her clients, obsessed with some fatal attraction you hear so much about these days."

"I don't think so, doc." Gil stopped rocking and his gaze shifted to Valerie's worried eyes. He urged her with his look and a slight hand gesture to tell Geoffrey the reason for her seemingly senseless attack. Val's gaze dropped to the floor and she shook her head vaguely, refusing to cooperate.

Geoff hadn't noticed these signals pass between the couple. He walked over to the window, pulled the slats of the mini-blind down to peer out onto the street, appearing in deep thought, then returned to Valerie. "Pack enough clothes to last a few days, Val. I'm taking you back to Stoneybrook with me."

Before she could reply, Gil shot up to his full five foot, ten inch height. "I don't think that's a good idea."

Geoffrey whirled around, more than a little annoyed with this cop. "Well, I do. My mind's made up, Ellis. I appreciate you replacing her lock, but what do you expect her to do now? Stay prisoner up here while her assailant's free to live his life as he pleases?"

Gil hesitated, not wanting to betray Val's confidence, but

knowing he had to make Geoffrey somehow understand. "Look, it seems this guy knows a great deal about Valerie's activities. He knew that she was going to the Baxter woman's apartment and waited for her there, to shoot her. And he knew it was safe to let himself inside here when she left to report this at the station."

"Which means, he was following her."

"Precisely. Who's to say he's not out there now, waiting to follow you to your place? He probably knows your schedule, and when you go off to work, guess what? He enters Stoneybrook."

Geoffrey stared at him, not knowing whether to laugh at Gil or accuse him of being an alarmist. Instead, he assured him, "Valerie won't be alone for a moment. My son is there as well as my live-in housekeeper. And until after the new year, so will mother."

"I'm so glad you pointed that out to me, doc, that makes all the difference in the world." Gil tossed his hands up, scarcely believing the naïveté of this man. "Two older women and a kid! Now that's security!"

"What can you offer her, Ellis—twenty-four-hour police protection?"

Gil's eyes swept up to the overhead fan and he studied for a moment. "You know, you just might have stumbled on to the best idea yet. It so happens, I have some time coming. I could take a working vacation and be Val's own personal bodyguard."

Geoffrey's eyes blazed. He'd about had it with this overbearing cop. "And who would protect her from you? I doubt if you could be alone with this woman for an hour without your hormones raging out of control. No, thanks. I'd rather take my chances with the man that's stalking her."

Valerie saw Gil's jaws clench and his fists knot. She jumped between them, placing a hand upon each man's chest. She was well aware of Geoffrey's distaste for Gil, but his blunt remarks were out of character and totally uncalled for. And she knew Gil's easy-go-lucky personality did have a limit, especially where this pediatrician was involved.

"Please, let's stop it right now before this gets totally out of hand. We have to concentrate on getting this guy and not fighting one another. Taking everything into consideration, I think the best course of action for me is to go to Stoneybrook for a few days. And Gil, you put your efforts into arresting this man so I'm free to return to a normal life."

The young officer looked for a moment as though he were going to hotly argue the point, but turned instead and grabbed his leather jacket off the back of the sofa and slipped it on. But when he reached the door, he turned to look at the woman he loved and the man who stood between them.

"I think you're making a very serious mistake, Faraday, but I can't force my will on Val. We're dealing with a dangerous personality here, possibly even a psychopath. When you finally come to terms with that, I think you'll agree that as a trained officer, I'm in a much better position to protect her than you are. And one more thing," he said, jabbing Geoffrey in the shoulder once with his finger. "This bull about me being a threat to her if we'd be alone is extremely offensive to me. She's perfectly safe and she knows it. Just ask her."

"Good-bye, Lieutenant," Geoffrey said curtly.

Gil's angry and hurt eyes rested on the quiet woman now. "I'll be keeping in touch. Remember what I told you last night, Val. Your prince may not be coming on a white horse, but he sure isn't coming wearing a white lab coat either. If you should change your mind about anything, I'm only a phone call away.'' And with that, he left, slamming the door behind.

''What the devil is he babbling about now?'' Geoffrey muttered. And before she could think of a face-saving way to explain, he jumped to another subject, though his thoughts were still very much taken up with Gilbert Ellis. ''You know, for a moment there I actually thought he was going to hit me.''

''No, he wouldn't have, but I could understand that he might have wanted to. You assaulted his character, Geoff. You've got him pegged all wrong.''

''Do I?'' he asked, his voice softening as his eyes dropped to meet hers. He gathered her hand and ran his finger over the diamond he'd recently slipped on her finger. ''This says you're spoken for, a fact he consistently ignores.''

His eyes slipped to the thin scars on the back of her hand. *Go on, kiss it*, Val urged in her thoughts. She held her breath, watching those full sensuous lips which were quick to kiss her face but never her hands. Gil was going to kiss them without giving it a second thought last night, until she stopped him. She tilted her head, watching Geoff's hesitancy. His eyes swept up to meet hers and they crinkled in a smile. With his dark, wavy hair and strikingly clean olive complexion, Valerie thought he would make a magnificent prince . . . accept for those glasses. But then a princess didn't have scars on the backs of her hands either.

''Better pack your bags now.''

He released her hand without affirming her fragile ego with that desired kiss. And for the moment, the spell was broken.

Red barns decorated with colorful hex signs of the Pennsylvania Dutch flashed by as Geoff and Val drove deeper into the country toward Stoneybrook. It was a tranquil scene, but it had little effect on the emotionally torn young woman. Before they had left her apartment, Geoff was insistent about checking her wound and putting on a new dressing. He seemed pleased with the way it looked, and like Cantrell, he expected no future problems.

"I have some great news to share with you, Valerie," he said, breaking the silence. "I recently got word that the Chief of Pediatrics is retiring and Hoffman and I are being considered for the position."

Val's face brightened. "Congratulations!"

"Thanks, but that's a bit premature," he said, taking his eyes off the road a moment to look at her. "I'm going up against some pretty stiff competition. Hoffman's ten years my senior and he's good, really good. Of course, the fact that I have a spotless record is in my favor. No malpractice suits amid a thriving practice is nothing to be taken lightly these days. But that Karney's the Chief of Staff and he's known to probe into the private lives of his people to see if there's anything which will later cause embarrassment."

Geoffrey took his hand off the wheel for a moment and placed it on hers to give it a quick, heart-felt squeeze. "How I want this position! Dad coveted it for himself, but for some reason it always eluded him."

"He would be very proud that you're under consideration. I know I am!" she assured him, then thought, *But that Karney . . . would he stop with just examining Geoffrey's background? Would he consider the prospective wife as well?* It didn't seem fair if he did.

The young doctor guided his luxury car through the red-painted covered bridge. Tires rumbled over its dipping wooden floor, then they emerged out into the brilliant sunshine once more. Val could never forget the day they'd met. What a disaster! Though she'd lived in the area all her life, she still managed to get lost on the winding back roads.

Because she'd been concentrating on finding a certain road, she didn't see the jogger until the very last moment. She missed the man, but not the water-filled pothole. Muddy water splashed up, spraying his white shorts and black jersey. Val didn't know what to do—stop and apologize or drive on to meet her new client. She chose the latter, only to find to her chagrin, her prospective client came stomping and grumbling into the house, griping to his housekeeper, Madelyn Price, about that crazy woman driver who'd splashed him. Somehow, everything turned out all right. She'd gotten the job in spite of their rocky beginning, and now she was getting the man as well. So why wasn't she delirious with happiness? Buddy Saget was why: that dark smudge in her past, looming up to threaten her future and disturb her present.

After driving another mile through woods on the left side and a lazy flowing creek on the right, the terrain gave way unexpectedly to a well cared for lawn, dotted with deciduous trees. Now you could see the house, but in the summer months, the leaves mostly hid it from view. Val straightened as they approached. Originally part brick and part frame, it had the appealing uniformity of rustic wooden siding. Geoff had told her the land had been in his late wife's family for generations. Her grandfather had willed it to her, Jessica, his favorite grandchild.

Geoffrey pulled up the circular driveway, but didn't enter the attached three-car garage. He took Val's suitcase in one hand, and with a guiding hand across her back he ushered her up the wide steps and onto the long porch. The name Stoneybrook was rustically routed out on a piece of wood over the massive front door.

"Madelyn!" he called out as soon as they entered. He helped Val out of her coat and hung it up in the foyer closet. A middle-aged woman in a flour-smudged gray sweatsuit emerged from the back room. Her friendly, round face wreathed in a grin when she saw them.

"Hello, Valerie. The doctor told me you'd be coming over for dinner." Her eyes dropped to the suitcase at his feet.

To answer her unspoken question, Geoffrey quickly explained, "Valerie's been receiving harassing phone calls over the weekend, and on top of that, her apartment was broken into. I thought it best she spend a couple days here with us."

"Of course." Madelyn turned to Val and concern replaced her motherly grin. "Are you all right, dear?"

"She's fine, Maddie, and I want to do my part to keep her that way," Geoffrey spoke up, not giving Val a chance to admit she'd also suffered a flesh wound.

Valerie's smile was a baleful one. "I've had my lock changed this morning but getting an unlisted number is out of the question. I must be accessible to my clients."

Geoffrey slid a protective arm around her shoulder, avoiding the bandage. "Is Mother upstairs?"

Madelyn tore her eyes from Valerie's strained features and shook her head. "No, she went out for a walk, but she should be back shortly."

"I must speak to her about this unexpected development. Meanwhile, I'll get Valerie settled."

The housekeeper nodded, but wondered as she returned to the kitchen if there weren't more to this than they were letting on. Their grim expressions spoke louder than their words.

Chapter 6

Val followed Geoffrey up the stairs, past the cozy reading nook to the room at the front of the house. Definitely feminine with its pinks and whites, it was a delight to her artistic eye. It wasn't the first time she'd seen it, of course. Geoff had given her a tour of the estate when she came to convert the antique shop into a sunroom and gallery and change the formal living room into a more inviting great room. This particular area, which she had taken such a liking to, had been Jessica's during her frequent visits to her grandparents.

"I just love this!" she exclaimed, the little girl within bubbling to the surface. She ran her hand along the gentle curves of the oak sleigh bed. It was a bed fit for a princess. *Oh Val*, she mentally admonished, *there you go again. Get out of your dream world, you don't need it anymore!*

Geoffrey set her luggage aside. "I knew it enchanted you, that's why I chose it for you. That and," he laughed, "it's the last available room. The Faraday inn is now full. Want a hand with the unpacking?"

"No. I'll be through in a jiffy."

"All right then, come down when you're finished. Mother should have returned by then and I'm anxious for her to meet you. Heaven knows, I've bragged enough about you."

Valerie watched as he disappeared out the open door, then turned to the task at hand. Not knowing how long she'd be a guest at Stoneybrook, she had brought an assortment of clothing. Val laid a skirt and blouse aside with the intention of changing into them shortly. She wanted to look her best when she met Mrs. Faraday. In a matter of minutes, she had these hanging up in the armoire. Then she placed her lingerie in the paper-scented drawers.

Valerie reached for her brush and began to stroke it through her thick hair. And as she did this, her thoughts, never far from Buddy Saget, began to turn to him once again; Gil just had to find Saget with the least amount of delay before Saget totally wrecked her life. He just had to!

In that moment, something hit Valerie's arm, scaring her badly. She whirled about, choking back a scream to find Ryan Faraday standing there in a cowboy hat and holster with a toy gun. He pointed the latter at her chest, all set to shoot another suction cup dart at her.

He pulled the trigger, but this time she was ready for it and jumped aside. "Ryan!" she yelled, brandishing the brush in the air. "Don't you ever, ever point a gun at anyone! Do you hear me?"

He'd heard; his gleeful face crumbled, and a moment later he went wailing from the room.

She groaned, thinking, *Here we go again, another clash with the pint-sized barbarian!* Hesitating only a moment, she scurried after his screaming form.

"Valerie should be down any minute, Mother," Geoffrey said as they entered the great room. "She's really anxious to meet you." He drew back his sleeve to see the timepiece. "I wonder what's keeping her. I sent Ryan up several minutes ago to get her."

As though on cue, they heard a cry as the child came running down the stairs as quickly as his legs would carry him. Mother and son turned. Monica Faraday stretched out her arms to comfort the very distraught little boy, while Geoffrey's eyes grew enormous behind his glasses. Val was right on Ryan's heels, pleading with him to slow down before he fell.

His mouth slid open in disbelief at the sight of his fiancée's state of disarray. "Valerie! Your hair!"

She stopped abruptly, noticing the two surprised adults standing in the center of the room. Her free hand went to her head and it was then that she realized that one side had been brushed at a crazy angle. She must resemble a banshee!

"Oh!" she cried out in equal surprise as she tried to smooth it down, while Ryan screamed all the while, hiding behind his grandmother's woolen skirt. Then she remembered the brush in her hand. She quickly laid it on the console and faced the gaping pair.

Geoffrey found his voice first and though his look of deep disappointment remained engraved on his face, his tone was amazingly calm. "Valerie, I want you to meet my mother, Monica Faraday. Mother, this is Valerie Quinn."

The hand that Val extended almost shook with trepidation. What an awful first impression to leave her future in-law with. "Hello, Mrs. Faraday. I assure you, I don't usually make such a noisy entrance. I mean . . . I didn't realize you were here, in this room."

Monica allowed Val the courtesy of a smile and accepted the hand of friendship extended to her. "My son told me you were a lively one. It appears he wasn't kidding.'' She shifted her gaze to him in an affronted manner.

Ryan screamed on.

Geoffrey whirled around and snapped at the only one he felt he could unleash his humiliation on. ''What the dickens are you howling about now, Ryan!''

''Val's . . . go . . . gonna hi . . . hit me,'' he stuttered with a shuddering sob.

''You're wrong, Ryan. I had no intention of hitting you.''

''A natural mistake, Miss Quinn,'' Monica pointed out, ''considering you were coming at the boy with your hair brush.''

''It's not how it looks, really,'' Valerie said, close to tears herself. Steeling herself, she turned to face Geoffrey, then froze for a second. She'd never seen his cheeks so flushed, his brow so furrowed. Bad sign. Gulping a deep breath, Valerie hurriedly began to explain. ''Ryan flew into my room and scared me half to death. He shot one of those projectiles at me. I suppose I overreacted and yelled at him, but when I tried to apologize and explain my feelings, he ran away, screaming.''

''Did the suction cup hit you?''

''It did, on my upper left arm,'' she said, looking him direct in the eye.

He stared at her for a moment, still trying to deal with his disappointment. ''Mother had cleaned out a few of the things she's been saving since I was a boy. The felt hat, gun, and holster were among those items she wanted to pass down to my son. He never had a toy gun before. He's only five, Val; he couldn't have realized the emotional impact his role-playing would have on you.'' He picked the little boy up. ''Come on partner, you and I will have a man-to-man talk about this misunderstanding over milk and cookies. Meanwhile, your grandmom and Val can get acquainted.''

It amazed Valerie how quickly those tears were forgotten at the prospect of cookies. She wanted to suggest that she and Monica join them . . . that now was not the time to be left alone to get to know each other. But Geoff walked away before she could stop him, leaving the two uncomfortable women to muddle through as best they could. Valerie forced a smile as she tried in vain to think of something clever and witty to say, but brilliant conversation eluded her. Finally, she waved her arm toward the sofa. "Shall we?" And without waiting for a reply, the younger woman led the way.

Val felt like strangling Geoff for leaving her in such an awkward position. She looked at the woman once more, who looked back at her. Though Monica's eyes were piercing and dark and her chin square and slightly cleft, there was little other resemblance between mother and son. Her casually styled hair was light brown, not dark like Geoffrey's. Her ears and her teal sweater were adorned with decorative Indian jewelry, and her face was tastefully made up for a woman Val judged to be in her late fifties.

"I like what you've done with this room." The older woman finally spoke, breaking the strained silence between them.

"Thank you. It was a challenge, yet I had great fun doing it. I tried to create an unpretentious scheme as opposed to something on the opposite end. For instance, the fabrics have a farmhouse flavor with cottons and linens instead of silks or damasks."

Val folded her hands over her crossed knee and went on, hoping to impress upon this woman that she was an intelligent individual, which was what Geoffrey initially saw in her. "We decided to keep a few of Jessica's antiques, such as the child's bicycle over there," Val said, nodding toward the black-painted bike. "But most of the antiques, as you probably know, went to other dealers and . . ."

"You resemble her."

Valerie blinked, surprised by the comment. "Jessica?"

"Yes. Surely you've seen her pictures—there are a number of them in the house. As a matter of fact, there's one over on the mantle."

Val didn't have to turn to look; she was familiar with the photograph to which Monica referred. Jessica and her brother Adrian stood beside the pool in the back of the house, their smiles frozen for future generations. Well, hers was anyway. The man in the picture didn't appear very happy. There was something about him that disturbed Valerie, but she couldn't put her finger on just what that elusive something was. She sensed she had seen him before, and perhaps she had. Cedarcrest, after all, was a small town. Val was ready to query the woman about Adrian, but Monica's thoughts were still on her former daughter-in-law, and she began to speak before Valerie could.

"Jessie had auburn hair too, but then, my son's always been partial to women with that color hair." Her expression saddened as she unconsciously began to toy with her exquisite turquoise necklace. "No matter how old they are, you still grieve when your children are hurting. It's been a horrible two years for Geoffrey. First, Jessie had that fatal aneurysm. It hit Geoff especially hard. And being a physician, he wrongfully blames himself, feeling he could have saved her, somehow. I was grateful for the close friendship he had with Alexandra and John. Then John so unexpectedly died of a heart attack. He was so young."

"I know. Alex is still having a hard time dealing with it."

"Geoffrey understood exactly what she was going through and he offered his shoulder for Alex to cry on and his time to help Megan ease through the loss of her father. He's very fond of that little girl.''

''Yes. I've noticed right from the onset that he's a natural with kids. I suppose that's why he's so good at what he does.''

Though Monica agreed heartily, that intense sadness did not leave her eyes. ''I was so hoping that this cycle of heartache was over, but it wasn't. Corinne's baby died from sudden infant death syndrome in this very house during a birthday party for Megan. They say things happen in threes. I hope to heaven it's all over now, Miss Quinn. I so hope it's over.''

''Me too. And call me Valerie, please. If all goes according to plan, I will be your new daughter-in-law this spring.''

A vague smile touched the woman's lips. ''You know, there for awhile I was guessing who it would be—Alexandra or Corinne. I know they both have very deep feelings for my son. Are you aware of that, Valerie?''

Val reflected a moment. ''I don't have a problem with Geoffrey having close friends of the opposite sex so long as their relationship remains platonic. I trust him as I trust Alex and Corie too.''

''You're more generous than I would be.''

Though Monica resisted making any personal jabs, Valerie felt the older woman was not above hurting her by casting a shadow over the integrity of their friends. Val wasn't naive. Val knew the two women liked Geoff and if he were not engaged, perhaps they would vie for his affection, but not now. Now her only real problem was Buddy Saget and she couldn't help but wonder just how much Geoff had told his mother about her nemesis. Considering his strong sense of privacy, Geoffrey probably told her no more than he had to.

Ryan got over his anger with Val and returned to his posture of indifference toward her. How badly she wanted to bond with the boy and change the wicked stepmother image he had of her. It seemed everything she did was wrong. Desiring to spend some quality time with him before supper, she suggested they crayon together. After several minutes of coloring, he presented his artwork to Val for her approval. She was deeply hurt by the results. It was an illustration of a man, woman, and boy. He'd crayoned ugly lines across the woman's hands and Val, once again, lost her temper with the little boy.

"Ryan! This is cruel. You don't make fun of people."

Wailing for his grandmother, he raced out of the room. And once more, she followed after him, not wanting to cause a scene, but knowing she would. And again, she found herself apologizing to the trio. Geoffrey told her in a controlled tone that she was just being too sensitive, and that Ryan never meant anything malicious by it. To keep the peace, she agreed and promised she'd try harder in the future, while Monica gave her son that kind of look that clearly said, "What were you ever thinking when you chose this woman?"

"Your mother doesn't like me," Valerie complained. They'd tucked Ryan in bed and were now seated in the den, sipping hot chocolate. "Everything I do is wrong."

"You're trying too hard, Val. And in spite of what you may think, Ryan did not intend to sabotage your feelings. The illustration was one of a father, mother, and son—a family. You should feel honored that he put your personality into the picture as he sees you."

"As he sees me?" she repeated, feeling like something out of a sideshow.

"You're just tired. You get a good night's sleep and I guarantee you'll feel like a new woman in the morning. Go on now, doctor's orders," he said, relieving her of her mug.

Thinking he was probably right, she rose and started toward the door. As Geoff took a last sip from his own mug, the phone rang. He asked Val, who was walking by it at the time, to answer it.

"I hope it's not an emergency," he muttered, rising. "I'm kind of tired myself."

Valerie heard a click on the other end, then the sound of a crackling fire. Her heart began to pound and she gasped, her horror-filled eyes turning to the advancing physician. She listened, mesmerized by the noisy truck and then the music which grew in crescendo. And lastly, that gunshot. Val smacked the palm of her hand down on the table. "Stop it! Why are you doing this to me! Why!"

Geoffrey grabbed the receiver from her and heard, "I'm watching you, Kaylene. I know you're with Faraday . . . "

"Who the devil is this!"

The slamming phone clicked heavily in his ear. He held the receiver away and stared at it mutely for a moment, before placing it in its cradle. His eyes, filled with confusion, lifted to the woman before him.

She was shaking her head in mental rejection. "He knows! But how can he? How can he possibly know that I'm here!"

"He must have followed us from your apartment, just like Ellis suggested he might." Geoffrey's instincts were alerted. He didn't like Val's color and when he placed his hand on her shoulder, he could feel her trembling. "You'd better sit down, Valerie, before you collapse."

"No." She shoved his hand away. "There's no place I can hide from that man, don't you understand that!" Valerie didn't want to succumb to tears, but she did. This was the

topping on a perfectly lousy day . . . that very last straw.
"Geoff, please help me. I can't take much more of this, I
really can't."

Without a word, he went to the closet and lifted his satchel
from off the top shelf. Pulling herself from growing hysteria,
Val watched as he began to fill the syringe.

She drew in a deep breath. Of all people for her to become
hysterical around! Alex or Corie might have shaken her,
Gil would have held her tightly, whispering words of assurance, but not this guy. Valerie groaned. "Geoffrey, I
don't need that."

"Yes, you do. Push your sleeve up."

She walked behind the sofa, placing it between herself
and him. Her eyes dropped to the hypodermic.

Geoff offered her a disarming smile. "Val, you're not
planning on being obstinate for me, are you?"

She tore her gaze from the dreaded object to look at him
now. "Yes. I'm not particularly fond of needles, but more
importantly, I don't need it. I promise you, I won't go
ranting and raving through the house like a madwoman.
Honest. I refuse to give your mother any more ammunition
than she already has," she finished with a weak smile.

Though he appeared doubtful, he did acquiesce to her
wishes. "Okay, I won't force anything on you, but if you
don't want to sleep, then I want to talk. He called you
Kaylene. Why?"

She hesitated, dreading this moment, if it ever came.
"When I was six . . . " She broke off, unable to tell him.
"I'm sorry, Geoff, but I'm just not able to discuss this right
now."

Valerie began to move toward the door, but he side-
stepped her, blocking her way. Reaching out, his fingers
settled on her bandaged arm and she grimaced. If he noticed,
his mind was too caught up in disturbing thoughts to con-

sider it. "You're not leaving this room until you tell me what on earth is going on around here. I'm fast running out of patience and I'm in no mood to be playing guessing games. You're going to be my wife, for goodness' sake! If that doesn't give me the right to know, then I don't know what does."

It was harder than she ever imagined—much harder than it was when she bared her soul to Gilbert. Gil had sat beside her and let her speak, never interrupting, while Geoffrey paced in front of her, breaking into her story countless times. It reminded her of an interrogation, and though he kept his tone low, Val was hurt to see the shock and dismay which frequently crept into his expression. By the time she was finished, she was crying softly, her face hidden in her hands.

Geoffrey didn't try to console her and when she lifted her head, he was standing, one hand on the mantle, the other on his hip, staring at her with a look that wounded and wilted her to the very core of her being. "How could you do this to me, Val?" he finally said. "Or should I call you Kaylene? My gosh, I don't even know you!"

As she rose to her feet, her chin tilted defiantly. "The feeling's mutual, Geoffrey. I don't know you either, and quite frankly at this point, I don't care to. I'll leave first thing in the morning. Place the blame entirely on me. Tell your mother that in view of our clashes today, I've decided I wouldn't make an acceptable stepparent for your son." And with that said, she began to walk toward the door.

"No!" he said, grabbing her by the arm.

Tears pooled in Valerie's eyes. "Will you please stop doing that, Geoffrey, it hurts."

He released her instantly and took a step backward, raising his hands in an almost apologetic gesture. "I know I'm not handling this very well, but try to see my side of it too, Val. This has hit me like a bolt of lightning out of a clear blue sky. Here I find the woman I'm about to marry is the daughter of a man whose criminal act has left three people dead and . . . and now, twenty years later, the surviving son is out to seek his revenge. How in the name of common sense do you expect me to react to that?''

"By being supportive—like Gil was.''

"Gil,'' he sighed, running a hand across his furrowed brow. "Who else knows?''

"Only the police, because they have to. Geoffrey,'' she lifted a determined finger, "I've lived with this hanging over my head most of my life. I thought I'd broken free of it. And now, my past has caught up. I'm a victim here too, and I'm tired of paying for what they say my father did. I'm not taking it anymore. It's got to stop. Now!''

At last Geoffrey reached out and gathered her to him. "Forgive my insensitivity, Val. Somehow, I don't know just how yet, we'll work through this. We will.''

Though Valerie wrapped her arms around his waist and clung to him, there was no sense of security, no feeling of true acceptance. He never once told her he loved her. And when she lifted her head to look into his brooding face, she couldn't help but wonder if he were considering how all this could hurt his chances of getting that coveted job as Chief of Pediatrics.

Chapter 7

Geoffrey entered Valerie's room early the next morning, immaculately dressed in gray trousers, tie, and a white shirt. But Val thought he looked tired, as though he hadn't slept very well. "I'm glad to see you're up and ready to begin your day. Did you have a good night's rest?"

"I've had better," she admitted.

"Me too. I did a lot of soul searching . . . a lot of pacing the floor as I tried to discover the answers to difficult questions."

"And I bet one of those questions heavy on your mind is, do I really want to marry this woman? Geoffrey, if you want out, I'll understand."

"But I don't want out. I need you, Val, sometimes more than I care to admit," he confessed with a languid smile. "And I'm sorry I hurt you last night by the cutting things I said."

"I guess we both said things we really didn't mean."

He nodded, then changed the subject. "Something un-expected came up. Maddie's daughter called and wants her to fly out to Cincinnati for Christmas. She feels guilty about leaving at a time like this, but I told her we'll be okay. It's not as though you'll be alone. Mother's here."

Valerie agreed that there would be no problem.

"Another thing," he went on soberly. "I think we should hire a private eye to track down this Saget character."

"But Geoff, Lieutenant Ellis is looking into the matter. I'm sure he'll be making an arrest very soon."

"I don't know, Val. I think it's a bad idea that he's handling your case. You are, after all, an old girlfriend, and in light of that I don't think he should be so personally involved. It could hinder his performance. It falls in the same category as a physician operating on a family member or a close friend—it shouldn't be done."

"You're jealous," she gently accused. When he only stared back at her, she calmly continued, "Geoff, you're very compatible with Alex and Corie. I have no problem with that, although I suppose I could if I let myself dwell on it."

"That's different. I'm not blind, Val. I see the way he looks at you . . . like some hungry wolf about to devour a helpless lamb."

Valerie bit her lip to keep from laughing at his outrageous analogy. He noticed and smiled, but his next statement sobered her quickly. "Val, I want us to get married as soon as possible. We can get our bloodwork done this morning, then go right to the courthouse to apply for our license. My associate can cover for me at the office until I return."

"What's the big rush, Geoffrey?"

"This difficult situation we find ourselves in, that's what. I want to take care of and protect you, and I can do that best if you're my wife." He tenderly caressed her cheek.

"I know every girl's dream is a big wedding with all the trimmings and I'm not saying we can't have that—later. But for now I think we should have a quick, private ceremony with Mother as our witness. If you go along with my wishes, I'll make it up to you, I swear I will. You'll never be sorry you did."

Valerie had sat quietly beside Geoffrey on the way to the courthouse, unsure and confused about how fast things were moving. She placed her sprawling signature on the necessary papers, then walked back down the steps of the tall building and to the car. Sooner than she anticipated, she'd be Valerie Faraday, wife of the debonair Doctor Faraday. So why wasn't she bouncing on the seat, ecstatic with joy? She had a pretty good reason why.

Geoffrey, always conscious of good manners, opened the car door for her to slide in. Once seated, she thanked him, her eyes shifting past him to a vehicle parked across the street.

It couldn't be! She blinked, hoping her eyes were playing tricks on her, but there it was—a dark pickup truck, and inside sat a bearded man with a stocking cap. The instant Geoff placed the key in the ignition, Val placed her hand over his. "Wait!"

Geoff looked at her curiously. "What is it?"

"That's him, the man that's been harassing me." She noticed his eyes dart up and down the street and she specified, "In the truck directly across from us. My gosh, Geoff, he must have followed us here!"

"I'm going to settle this here and now!" he said grimly, opening the door, but Val lunged and caught his sleeve.

"Don't go, Geoff, please! He's probably got a gun."

"I'm going over to him," he said stubbornly, disengaging

her clutching fingers. "If he pulls away, try to get his license plate number."

"But Geoff . . . " Then she broke off, knowing he was determined and no amount of pleading would dissuade him. Valerie rummaged in her handbag for a paper and pen. Poised and waiting, she expected the stranger to speed off when Geoffrey approached, but he didn't.

Val lowered her window, hoping to catch bits and pieces of their conversation, but there was no sound except that of the constant flow of traffic along Court Street. About the time she thought she could stand it no longer, Geoffrey straightened from his position at the window and walked swiftly back to her.

The young woman watched anxiously as he slammed the door. His cheeks were flushed and she wondered what had happened now. He didn't keep her wondering very long.

"That was Pete Saunders, father of two of my patients," Geoffrey explained in a disgruntled tone. "He came up to get a dog license and thought he'd recognized me when I got to the car. He was looking over at me to make sure. At me, Val." He jammed the key back in the ignition switch. "You're going to have to get a handle on your nerves, Valerie. I almost made a fool of myself, rushing over there like that to pull the guy out of the car. Thank heaven I recognized him before I put my thoughts into actions!"

Val sank back in the leather seat, her eyes stinging with unshed tears. "I'm sorry, Geoff. I'll try harder in the future." It seemed she was saying that a lot of late.

"This weather sure is fickle," Madelyn complained as she rinsed the last plate and set it on the drainer. "The mercury's going up and down like a yo-yo."

"It's gotten awfully foggy out there. Let's hope it lifts before your plane takes off."

"I feel guilty about leaving you alone, yet I haven't seen my new grandbaby and he's three months old now."

"Of course you want to see him, and you're not leaving me alone, Maddie. Either Geoffrey or Monica will be here. Speaking of my future in-law, where is she?"

"She and Ryan are out building a snowman. My, how she loves that little boy!"

The sigh Valerie expressed at that moment was one which caused the housekeeper's gaze to linger on Val's longing face. "What's the matter, dear?"

"Ryan. I wonder if he'll ever accept me. I try so hard, but everything I do turns out wrong. We had two serious falling-outs yesterday, and then today we had a mild clash of wills. I wanted Ryan to finish his meal before delving into his dessert. Monica said, 'Geoffrey didn't always eat all his veggies and it didn't hurt him.' I looked over at Geoff for support and he kept right on eating, pretending he didn't notice, but I know he did."

"Oh, honey," Maddie slipped a mothering arm around Val's waist and gave it a comforting squeeze. "I know it's frustrating, but Ryan's suffered a very serious loss. He and his mother were close and her death has left a big empty space in his life. Now, he's shifted his affection to his daddy, and I think he's a trifle jealous of you stepping into the picture. I've noticed on many occasions how Geoffrey dotes on him, but it's not my place to say anything; after all, I'm just an employee. Don't you fret, Val. You'll be a fine wife and mother."

"Do you really think so?"

"Yes I do," she reaffirmed, looking Val in the eye. "I think you're the best thing that ever happened to either of them. And don't you let *her* make you feel different about it," she finished with a wink.

Valerie returned a conspiratorial smile before hanging the

tea towel on the rack. ''You know, I could use a walk about now.''

''Me too.''

When Valerie opened her mouth to tell her she should use her free time to pack, Maddie cut in. ''The doc would have my head if I let you wander around the property unescorted.'' She hesitated before adding, ''He felt I should know about that call last night, so he told me.'' Madelyn shook her head sadly as she went to gather her jacket and scarf. ''What a shame that the bad apples of this world are on the loose while decent folk must stay locked behind closed doors.''

A short time later, the two women walked down the drive and onto the road. They walked in companionable silence for a couple of minutes, when Val stopped short, wondering if her eyes were deceiving her. She took a few steps off the macadam and onto the ancient, snow-spotted lane. As she gazed through the fog to view the stark gray walls, an unsettling feeling caught her in its grip.

''What is this place, Maddie?''

Madelyn shoved her mittened hands in her pockets. Though she was aware of the ruins, she never gave them any particular thought. Her answer was a logical one. ''It appears to me to be a burned-out farmhouse. Why do you ask?''

Valerie didn't reply, but looked back down the lane, trying to visualize that fateful December night two decades ago. Could this rutted drive have once been the one they pulled up in her father's truck? She walked cautiously around to the front. A porch had long since rotted and collapsed; the height of the door bore testament to that. And when she peeked inside, it was with leery hesitancy, as though some specter from the past would suddenly appear. There was no floor, of course, only charred pieces of wood, partially covered with melting snow and underbrush. She tried to recall that huge living room, with its gaudy wallpaper of large pink flowers over a gray background. There was no remnant of paper now, of course. Not even an inner wall remained.

"Valerie, won't you please tell me what's wrong?" Madelyn pressed, concerned over the young woman's visible distress.

So Val told her the story and when she was finished, the housekeeper asked her if she thought this were the ruins of the Saget house.

"I don't know. Mother didn't keep any of the news clippings, and I did my best to forget about that night. I can't even remember the name of the road it was on. I was only six. Details like that aren't important to little kids."

Valerie sat on the base of the doorway and swung her legs over the side. This scorched shell was so small. The house of her childhood seemed so large—the entire living room could have been placed inside this whole area . . . or did it only seem that way because she was so young and impressionable? Valerie walked to where she remembered the kitchen to have been . . . the room where she ate doughnuts and drank milk with an up-to-then friendly Buddy Saget. But thirty minutes later, trapped in their living nightmare, he would try to destroy her. And, it appeared now, he was at it again. Why? Why now after all these years? She carefully picked her way through the debris to the doorway and climbed over.

Valerie surveyed the crumbling walls again, her gaze following the vegetation-choked chimney. At the top was a rusted wrought-iron initial, just barely visible. Swirls of misty fog obliterated, then revealed, the decorative *S. S.* for Simmons? Or for Saget?

Most of these years she hadn't given the Saget house fire

much room in her thoughts, and now since Friday evening, that's all she could think about. If only something more concrete would come back. Val ran her hand across her forehead as though to brush away the cobwebs of her dusty memory.

"Valerie," the housekeeper spoke, pulling her back to the present. "I don't think a walk was such a good idea. The dampness is getting to me."

Valerie pointed to the overgrown lane behind her. "Where does that lead?"

"It's a shortcut back to the house, but I don't think we should use it. You could stumble over downed branches or rocks hidden beneath the snow."

So the women began to walk single file in the direction from which they'd come. They were traveling up the driveway when the blast of a horn demanded their attention. Val turned; it was Gil. She told Maddie to go back to the house while she saw if he had anything new to report. And he had.

Val sat beside Gil in the patrol car and listened to what he had to say. "We ran a check on all three of the Sagets in the mug book. It's not turning out quite as I expected. It appears that Aaron's been behaving himself since he had that one-time scrape with the law. As a matter of fact, he owns a small restaurant in Reading. Claire was killed in a car crash six months ago. DUI. And Gary is serving time in Graterford for armed robbery."

"In other words, we're back to square one," Val concluded sadly.

"Not quite. Does the name Karl Saget mean anything to you?"

"Karl?" she repeated thoughtfully, then shook her head. "No, should it?"

"Buddy's real name is Karl. I dropped by the *Gazette*

this morning and your friend Alex and I went through all the material concerning the fire. As you can imagine, there had been a lot of coverage given to it, considering the time of the year it happened. You and Karl were taken to a neighbor's house to await the ambulance. Remember that?''

Val nodded. ''It was a big house. A lady with white hair brought me there. She wrapped some old terry towels around my hands to try and stanch the bleeding. It didn't help much.'' Sadness touched her heart as she concentrated on recalling the events of that shattering night. ''There were two other children in the house . . . a boy and a girl. They couldn't have been the woman's though, because she was an older lady. Perhaps they were her grandchildren.''

Gil drew her back to the present now. ''What were you doing walking along the road on a miserable day like this?''

''I felt I had to get out of the house, but I'm not sure it was such a good idea.'' She paused, not certain if she wanted to mention it, then did. ''We came upon an old ruin at the edge of the property. It's left me feeling so sad, and I'm not sure why.''

''I think you do, Val,'' he said directly, looking her in the eye.

She didn't flinch. ''Those articles you were reading, about the fire . . . it was on Old Denton Road, wasn't it?''

He reached for her hand now and held it. ''Yes. That kindly neighbor that took you into her home to wait was Frances Simmons of Stoneybrook. One of those little girls must have been Jessica, the Simmonses' granddaughter. She would grow up to eventually be the wife of Geoffrey Faraday. It's crazy sometimes, isn't it, how things work out?'' He looked at her profile now. She was staring at the dashboard, her back erect, her hand gripping his. ''Say something, Val. If you want to yell or scream, it's okay.''

She didn't do either, but her chin did tilt with fresh determination. "I'm all right. So, this is where it all happened, and now I've come full circle, back to the place where my life was unalterably changed. I can handle that." She gave his hand a parting squeeze before drawing it back on her lap. "What I can't handle is knowing that man is watching my every move. Every time the phone rings, I'm afraid to answer it, never knowing if the next sound I hear will be that awful tape. You have to find this Karl Saget, Gil, because I don't have a life until you do."

"I'm doing my best, Val." Yet, some instinct told him he might be leaning in the wrong direction. Why would a man wait twenty years to get even with a woman who was in no way responsible for what had happened? Unless he cracked. Gil knew that a person could lead a seemingly normal life and one day, something might happen—a divorce, a death of a mate or child, a job loss, anything—and lives rapidly disintegrated. Saget might be going back to the point where things began to unravel. He blamed his mother's death on Patrick Quinn. He couldn't touch the father, but he sure could wreak havoc on the daughter's life.

Leaning his elbow on the back of his seat, Gil rested his chin in the palm of his hand and asked casually if Val had told Faraday yet.

Val nodded.

"Everything?"

"Yes."

"And it didn't go very well," he guessed, noting her saturnine expression.

She sighed deeply, struggling with whether or not she wanted to discuss this personal matter with him, but Gil was a good listener. She related Geoffrey's bid for Chief of Pediatrics and told of Hoffman, the main obstacle standing between Geoff and the coveted position. "I planned to tell him on my own terms, preferably over a candlelight dinner. But it didn't work out that way and the timing couldn't have been worse.'' She visibly grimaced at the thought. ''We were alone in the den when the phone rang. It was *him*, Gil. He said he knew where I was.''

Gilbert straightened, surprised by what she was saying. ''What! He called you here? What exactly did he say?''

'' 'I'm watching you, Kaylene. I know you're with Faraday.' At that point, Geoffrey grabbed the phone, demanding to know who was calling. *He* hung up. I became a bit hysterical and Geoffrey wanted to sedate me. When I refused, he demanded to know what this was all about. I told him—not at all the calm atmosphere I wanted to create when I did relate this mess. We both said things we shouldn't have. Don't let anyone kid you—words can hurt. Oh Gil,'' Val fretted, slowly wringing her hands. ''*He* must have been watching my apartment and saw me leave with Geoff. You said he might.''

''Val, I wish you wouldn't be so stubborn about staying at my place until this thing is settled. I could make arrangements for Jenny and the kids to reside there. Brutus would be with you twenty-four hours a day for protection. I don't mean to drive even more fear into you, but this guy seems to get his kicks from terrorizing you. He'll probably call again.''

The young woman sat quietly for a moment, staring at her now-quiet hands. ''What about doing a wire tap?''

His smile was a condescending one. ''It's not that easy. I need a darn good reason to request one.''

''My life's being threatened. Isn't that reason enough?''

''It takes a court order, Val, and I can't get that overnight. Forget what you see in the movies; the laws being what they are, wiretapping is seldom used. Things must be done by a certain procedure or the evidence is thrown out of court.''

Then Gil brought up the matter of self-defense. He reviewed the moves he'd taught her when they were dating. But he could tell from her wrinkled nose that she didn't like what he was saying. He remembered that Valerie was squeamish about treading on a bug.

As the lawman watched Val alight from the car a few minutes later, he wondered about the twisted mind they were really dealing with and how far it was prepared to go.

Chapter 8

"There's a variety of casseroles in the freezer," Madelyn rattled on as she lingered in the entry. "And there's a pad on the counter by the fridge. Whenever you see you're gettin' low on an item, jot it down so I'm sure to get it when I do my marketing. The laundry's . . ."

"Maddie," Geoffrey cut in, suppressing his inclination to laugh as he placed two silencing hands on her shoulders. "We won't starve. I know from experience that the kitchen isn't foreign to either Mother or Val. If I run out of clean underwear, I know how to spin the dials on the washing machine. We'll be fine, really."

"About Valerie." Her voice dropped, not knowing just where the woman was, but knowing she didn't want her to overhear. "You keep a sharp eye on the girl, doc, and don't let that lunatic get his hands on her. No telling what he might do if he grabs her."

"He won't get near her, Maddie. I know both Alex and

101

Corie will spend time with Val when Mother or I can't. She'll be in the company of a responsible adult at all times. Trust me.''

The blast of a horn outside cut into their conversation. Maddie shook her tam-covered head. ''That son of mine was never known for his patience.''

''He's justified. If you don't get out of here soon, you'll miss your plane.''

''I'm goin'.''

''Have a nice trip and don't worry about us. We'll be just fine,'' he called after her. Geoff watched from the storm door until the car was out of sight. Then he turned to face Valerie, who had just entered the area. Fresh from the shower, her hair hung full and lustrous around the shoulders of her figure-hugging black body suit.

''Oh darn it, I wanted to give Maddie a good-bye hug.''

''You're a minute too late.'' His eyes ran admiringly over her once again. ''Don't you dare go out in public in that thing. I consider that for my eyes only.''

Val's hand settled guardedly over her low scalloped neckline. She certainly hadn't intended to dress in a provocative manner, but the faint disclosure of her cleavage told her she had. However, she reasoned, Geoff was a doctor and she assumed he wouldn't be the least affected by her favorite loungewear. ''Perhaps I should change.'' Her mood was on anything but romance.

''No, you shouldn't,'' he said, taking her by the hand and leading her to the great room. He lit the tree while she took her place on the sofa. Val really hadn't had a chance to talk to him since he'd come home from the office. Amid the hustle and bustle of Maddie's departure, they ate a hurried meal of chicken corn pie, then Geoffrey disappeared to take a shower. Later, she took hers and now she wanted to talk—to tell him about her newest revelation . . . that the ruins of the old Saget house bordered his property. He couldn't have known, or surely he would have told her this when she revealed her tragic story to him.

There was a gathering mound of gifts under the tree, but she realized her gifts to him and Ryan weren't counted among them. They were still home, unwrapped and lying on the top shelf of her bedroom closet—a closet she dreaded going to since she found that burned doll there. Val watched somewhat dismally as he went from the tree to start a cozy fire in the fireplace.

The sight of flames triggered thoughts of that night. It must have been to this very room that they had brought her. The tree was in front of the window where the sofa now sat, and Mrs. Simmons had rocked her while the other children sat quietly by, wide-eyed and staring at her wrapped hands. She couldn't see the burning house from that vantage point, but even so, they had closed the drapes to hide the orange glowing snow. She could hear the wail of the emergency vehicles racing—too late to save the old house and the victims inside. Mr. Simmons had brought Karl Saget to another part of Stoneybrook to wait for help. Once again, his hysterical cries echoed across time in her mind.

Suddenly Valerie became aware that Geoffrey had been speaking to her. She forced her eyes from the flames to the man's face. "Valerie, are you all right?" he was saying. "You look a million miles away."

Her smile was a languid one. "Not a million miles, Geoff. Same place, just a different time." She didn't explain further, nor did he ask her to. She had to think about something else other than her own past. Anything. One look at his expression told her exactly where his thoughts lay. So did that arm which slid around her shoulders.

"You make me feel like a kid holding a package with a sticker which reads, DO NOT OPEN UNTIL CHRIST-

MAS. And Valerie, I can hardly wait to tear off the wrapping to play with my brand-new toy.''

Val didn't know whether to laugh or gasp, scarcely able to believe he had actually said that. Gilbert yes, but the staid Geoffrey Faraday? "Shame on you, doc!" she half scolded. Her gaze slid to his lips and she tensed up, knowing what was about to happen. Was she crazy? she wondered. Or was it the stress she was constantly under which forbade her to melt in his arms? This man was every woman's fantasy, but her reality.

Geoff inched closer. "Considering the surprise I have for you tonight, I think we'll tuck Ryan in a little early. There are times a man just doesn't want to be disturbed."

His lips had just begun to brush hers when Monica breezed in. Geoffrey froze for a second, then drew back, clearly annoyed that his romantic advances were interrupted. And by the other woman in his life at that—his mother. Monica stopped short, realizing that she had inadvertently walked into a very private moment. Her cheeks burned with sudden embarrassment . . . or was it resentment? Valerie wasn't sure. The young woman drew back from his embrace, not knowing what she felt other than confusion and, oddly, gratitude. At that moment, the running dynamo named Ryan dashed into the room. Geoff grunted as the little boy landed square on his lap in a position which hurt him.

The child ignored Val as he looked up into his father's face. "Let's play with my train set now."

"No."

He leaned back, indignant and surprised that his normally doting father would deny him anything. "Why not?"

"Because I'm spending time with Valerie right now. She's a part of my life too and you'd better well get used to that."

The lad's lower lip pouted out and his brows gathered in a frown identical to the one his father was wearing. Big brown eyes shifted to meet Val's and they stayed. Never did she see such scorn and resentment in a child so young.

Valerie slumped back on the sofa thinking, *Here we go again!* She was conscious of the ring of the doorbell and of Monica's grateful and hasty exit. Val glanced at Geoffrey, who was glowering like a kid who'd just been denied getting something he really wanted. "Geoff, it's okay. Perhaps it would be a good idea if you two ran that train a few times around the track."

"What!" He set the youngster down rather hard. "Val, aren't you the one who's always telling me I give in to his every whim? And now, when I am taking your side, you're sticking up for Ryan? I don't get it."

"I'm not taking sides," she insisted uncomfortably, knowing the very last thing she wanted to do was argue and show disunity in front of this child. "There will be plenty of time for us to be together after Ryan's tucked in for the night."

"No," he repeated stubbornly. "He's not getting his way this time."

Val looked helplessly from father to son, each glaring at her for his own reason. It was ridiculous having a verbal altercation over something like this.

"Hi, everyone!"

The tense trio turned to the laughing small group which had just entered. Corinne stopped short, looking from one flushed face to the other. "Oh dear! I think we popped in at the wrong time."

"I want Daddy to run the train set with me, but he'd rather kiss her. Yulk!" Ryan finished, and to Val's chagrin, he wiped his lips with the back of his hand. Suddenly, she had an almost irresistible urge to take that little barbarian over her knee.

But Alexandra found the whole scene rather amusing. "I'll remind you you said that in another ten years, sport."

Geoffrey subconsciously adjusted his glasses and forced a smile. "Hello, Alex and Corie. Your timing could have been better, yes, but you ladies know you're always welcome." His eyes shifted to Megan. "How's my favorite girl this evening?"

Meg dropped Corie's hand to race over to the man on the sofa and held up her doll for inspection. "Look what Val gave me, Doctor Geoff. Ain't she pretty?"

"She sure is!"

"I think she's got a fever, though. What do you think?"

"You talk dumb!" an ignored Ryan exclaimed. His father spoke his name warningly before taking the doll and laying it across his knees. He placed his fingers over its forehead. "Your baby have a name?"

"Uh-huh. Amanda."

Geoffrey hesitated a moment, caught by surprise at her reply, then went on. "I think Amanda's just fine, but you bundle her up when you take her out. And be sure to start off each day with a nice warm breakfast and a hug. Always remember that, Megan."

Ryan rolled his eyes, thinking his Dad must be pretty weird to be talking like that, but Megan didn't think so. She nodded soberly, filing this information away for when she grew up and the doll in her arms was real. "I'll be a good mommie."

"I'm sure you will be," he commented, his eyes shifting up to meet Alexandra's, "when you have such a good teacher."

Bored with it all, Ryan took a step closer to his peer. "You wanna see my train set, Meg?"

"Yeah!" And before another word was spoken, they tore out of the room together.

Corinne turned to Val. "How would you like to come along to the movies with us?"

While the young woman hesitated, Geoffrey spoke up, laying the doll aside. "Go ahead. It might do you good to get out."

It might, but she knew from the tone of his voice that he'd rather she wouldn't. "Thanks for the offer, Corie, but I'm kind of tired. I thought I'd spend a quiet evening with Geoff."

"Bring him along, and Ryan too. We'll make it a family film."

"Can we take a rain-check on that? I've got to admit, I'm rather bushed myself," said Geoff.

Satisfied they couldn't be talked into it, the women joined the couple on the sofa. They made small conversation about the Christmas decorations, then Corie broke the holiday mood with a deep sigh. "How I wish Amanda could have lived to see her first Christmas!" She shook her head sadly and went on, "Megan shouldn't have named her doll after my daughter."

"Oh, Corinne." Alex reached over and closed her hand on that of her friend. "Megan loved Amanda so much. I know she didn't name it after your child to hurt you, but rather to honor Mandy's memory. She thought the world of that baby of yours."

Geoffrey rose, and standing behind her chair, he laid a comforting hand on her shoulder. "I know it's difficult for you. Alex and I both empathize and understand what you're going through."

"No, you don't," she insisted, her wet eyelashes batting upward. "You lost your mates, not your children. Children shouldn't die before their parents . . . it isn't natural. I lost a part of me that I can never get back.''

"Corinne, listen," Geoffrey went on consolingly. "Someday you'll marry and probably have other children. I know they can't take the place of Amanda, but they will bring you joy. My goodness, woman, you're still young and attractive and you do have a lot to offer a man."

"Yeah," she said, wiping her tears away. "Only this time I'd better see the preacher before offering Romeo anything. Right?"

"It would be prudent," Geoffrey agreed. "Alex and I both know from experience, it's not easy being a single parent."

Once more Monica entered the room, took one look at the four solemn adults and halted in her tracks. "Don't tell me I walked in at a bad time . . . again?"

"No, not this time." Geoffrey gestured to the chair next to Corie's. "Sit down please, and join us."

So Monica, elegant as always in her full dark skirt, bulky sweater, and silver jewelry, seated herself. She offered each woman a quiet smile before turning to her son. "Well, dear, tell us all about your day."

That broke the ice and the intimate group sat around discussing matters of deep concern to Geoffrey—from the rise in suspected child abuse he was seeing among his young patients to the alarming escalation of "social diseases" in his older ones. At some point Alex drew back her cuff to check the time. "By golly, we missed our movie."

Corinne shrugged. "Doesn't matter. It's kind of nice to get together like this, and too, the kids seem to be enjoying themselves."

Geoff turned to Val. "Now, little lady, have I got a surprise for you."

"What is it?"

"You'll see in a couple of minutes. Mom, will you get the youngsters and bring them downstairs? I'm going to the kitchen for a moment, but I'll be right back."

Within five minutes, the children were gathered and Geoffrey reentered, carrying a silver tray of five long-stemmed glasses and two tumblers. He stopped before his mother first.

A bejeweled hand reached for one. "Champagne? What's the celebration, dear?"

"You'll hear all about it in a moment," he said with a secretive smile. Geoff handed the children their soda, with a warning not to spill any of it on the sofa, before joining Val, who was now standing alone by the fireplace.

When he handed her her glass, she whispered, "You received word that you have the position of Chief of Pediatrics, is that it?"

"No, that isn't it," he whispered back, then turned to face the women watching him so expectantly. "All right," he smiled, "I won't keep you guessing any longer. I must admit, what I'm about to say, I was going to say to Valerie first. But maybe it's better this way. Each of you are very near and dear to my heart, which I'm sure you already know. We've been through the worst of times these past two years; let's pray that's all behind us now." He paused and looked at each individual. When his eyes met his mother's she could keep silent no longer.

"Geoffrey, if you don't tell us what we're supposed to be celebrating this instant, so help me, I'll scream."

"I did have a lot of warm thoughts to convey, but I won't keep you in suspense a second longer . . . and I'll try to keep this short." He cleared his throat and tried to look appropriately dignified for the announcement.

"I request the honor of your presence here, at Stoneybrook, on Friday, Christmas Eve, when I take Valerie Quinn as my wife.'' He turned to Val and clinked his glass against hers. ''To us.''

His announcement caught the bride-to-be totally off guard and she could only blink up at him in surprise. *Married on Christmas Eve? He should have informed me first*, her mind screamed even if her lips did not, *instead of telling me with the others*.

Valerie was conscious of a small gasp, and wasn't sure which of the three women it came from, but the child's cry of protest she knew came from Ryan. Before anyone could stop him, he threw his tumbler to the floor and ran from the room, screaming as though his world had caved in. Geoffrey's hesitancy was only momentary, before he shoved his glass into Val's free hand, then rushed after him, calling his name sharply.

Valerie turned and looked at the three gaping women. Megan began to cry, not understanding what was going on, but knowing that something bad must have happened to affect Ryan that way. Alex retrieved the tumbler from her lest she drop hers too, then placed a comforting arm around her quaking shoulders. The look Monica shot Val bordered on contempt before she hastily excused herself to ''look after her boys.'' Then Valerie set the untouched glasses on the mantel, and without a word to the two remaining women, ran from the room.

Major, happy events in people's lives weren't supposed to plummet like this, she thought wildly as she ran into the kitchen. Val collapsed on one of the ladder-back chairs, pillowed her head in her folded arms on the table, and cried.

Valerie wasn't sure how long she sat there, letting those pent-up tears from the past few frustrating days spend themselves until she felt a hand on her shoulder. Someone spoke her name; she lifted her head and watched as Corinne drew out a chair to sit beside her. ''You okay?''

Val nodded mutely as she received a tissue from the box Corie slid in front of her. The receptionist chose her words carefully. "Geoffrey's intentions were good, Val, even if it seemed he didn't take your feelings into consideration. From the expression on your face, you appeared to have been taken in total surprise. But how could you have been? You did apply for a marriage license and have your blood tests done, so the next logical step would be the ceremony, right?"

The distraught bride-to-be blew her nose and wiped her eyes. "I know, but not a darn thing is going right. You saw Ryan's reaction. In his eyes I'm the epitome of the wicked stepmother. I can't do anything right where the boy's concerned. And if that's not bad enough, Geoffrey's mother barely tolerates me. As far as those two are concerned, I'm as welcome in this house as the flu."

"Poor Val," Corie sighed as she rubbed a comforting hand across the young woman's shoulder. "You should know that people like Monica are never satisfied with the girls their sons marry unless their last name is Vanderbilt or Rockefeller. Quinn or Greer just isn't going to cut it." She grinned. "Be glad for every mile between Baltimore and here that there is. But if you really get lucky, she'll retire to Arizona like I've heard her threaten to whenever she feels Geoff is slighting her."

The shaky corners of Valerie's mouth turned up and she actually laughed. Corie's hand slid back on her lap and she changed the subject abruptly. "What about your stalker? Are the police making any headway with him yet?"

"Gil believes it might be Karl Saget. He's trying to locate him for questioning."

Corinne hesitated. "I really wish someone besides Gil were handling this."

"Why? He's the best man on the force."

"I don't doubt that, but he's also a good friend and that, Val, could interfere with him doing his job. He might be too quick to make an arrest."

"No, not Gil." Valerie balled the damp tissue in her hand and slowly shook her head. "Oh Corie, this waiting game is just awful. I don't know if Geoff told you, but the stalker knows I'm here at Stoneybrook. He called last night. This couldn't be happening at a worse time, with Geoff up for that position. He wants it so badly. My nerves are shot," she confessed. "When we went for our license, I thought I saw the stalker outside the courthouse. A man in a pickup truck was staring at us and when I mentioned it to Geoffrey, he went over to him, ready to tangle with the guy if necessary. It turned out to be one of the fathers of his young patients. Geoffrey was really upset with me for jumping to wrong conclusions and I can't say that I blame him."

As Corinne listened, a thought came to her for the first time. Maybe she should tell Valerie about *him*. She wondered if Geoff had ever told her about his brother-in-law. "Valerie, I think . . ." She broke off, uncertain of the repercussions such an accusation would make.

The young woman looked curiously at Corinne, who suddenly seemed lost in deep thought. "What is it, Corie?"

"I think," she said cautiously, "we should be getting back to the others. Perhaps we can salvage some of this evening and celebrate your upcoming marriage. Valerie, you're getting the perfect man, you know that?"

Val nodded as she rose, pushing the chair back in place. Why then did she feel so heavy-hearted? It was hard to be enthusiastically optimistic when the generation before and after Geoffrey's took such a dim view of welcoming her into their family. Acceptance, Val knew, was of paramount importance if the smooth-running marriage she desired was to be brought to fruition.

Chapter 9

"Lieutenant Ellis dropped by," Val conveyed when they were finally alone, "to update me on the situation. The three Saget men I viewed in the mug book weren't any that were connected with the fire. He said he'd spent the morning with Alexandra, going over old articles devoted to the tragedy. The name of the boy . . . Buddy was really Karl—Karl Saget. Gil ran his name through the computer but there wasn't anything on him. Evidently he's been a law-abiding citizen." Val wasn't sure if that made her happy or not.

"So? He's not letting the investigation drop at that, I hope," Geoff commented, concern written across his face as he leaned forward, his elbows on his knees. "You know, I haven't given up the idea of hiring a private investigator."

"Hold off awhile, Geoff. With the help of local police agencies, Lieutenant Ellis will be checking up on every Karl Saget in the tri-county."

"What if he's no longer a resident in this state?" he

pointed out. "What if he just came back here with the intention of stalking, then after he's finished with you, he disappears, never to be heard from again?"

"If he's out of state, then I suppose they'll just have to extend their investigation. I know this much. Lieutenant Ellis will not give up until he finds this man."

Geoffrey smiled thinly. "I believe you're right about that. Ellis will keep this case open until he gets the guy who shot you, even if your stalker chooses never to come near you again."

Valerie took a deep breath, steeling herself to reveal what was bothering her even more. She rubbed the back of her neck, feeling the tension beginning to grip her. "Geoffrey, did you know that the Saget property bordered Stoneybrook and that the ruins are that of the Saget house?"

He straightened now, drawing his clasped hands back on his lap. "No, I didn't. But you must remember, Valerie, I wasn't raised in this area. Stoneybrook was Jessica's grandparent's estate. She never mentioned the fire that I can remember. I suppose she wasn't very familiar with it."

"Yes she was, Geoff, oh yes she was," Val contradicted as she rose and walked over to the wide brick fireplace. "Mrs. Simmons had brought me in here, wrapped my hands, and waited for the ambulance. Jessica was in this room too, at least I think it was she. Remember, when you first showed me the estate when I came to redecorate, I told you it seemed as though I'd been here before. Apparently I had been." Resting her hand on the mantel, Val gazed into the dying embers. "Geoffrey, I'm so afraid that my past will dictate my future."

The young physician walked over to her and laid his hand on her shoulder. Turning, she looked up into his troubled face, hoping he'd correct her and say, "our future." "I'll stand beside you Val, no matter what." His fingers slid down to her hand and he held it a moment, appearing to be deep in thought. He shook his head sadly and what he said next, Valerie could hardly believe.

"Of all times for this to happen! I certainly hope that Alexandra doesn't decide to resurrect the story, and she might, this being the twentieth anniversary of the conflagration. Perhaps I'd better call her and discuss it."

Val twisted her hand from his light grasp. "Yes, the timing is certainly lousy. My stalker could have had the courtesy to wait until you secured that coveted position."

His cheeks flushed as his eyes shifted to meet hers. "I didn't mean that the way it sounded, Val, but you must admit, the publicity is the last thing either of us wants. It would hurt your own business if it were brought to light that your father set a fire which snuffed out the lives of three people."

"I don't happen to think that he did."

"Evidently you're the only one who doesn't. You'll have to come to terms with the fact that he did, but whether it was intentional or not, you'll never know. Your father was a married man involved with another woman. Maybe he wanted out and she wouldn't let him go. It's possible he decided on impulse to free himself of her."

"By killing her and himself as well? That's asinine! You don't even know my father."

"I really don't think you do either, Val. You keep seeing the man as the victim in this . . . a position which Saget certainly doesn't take."

"I don't have to stand here and listen to this," she said, moving away, but he caught her by the arm.

"You must face the facts so you can accept, then bury them," he insisted, looking her directly in the eye.

She stared back defiantly. "What concerns me isn't so much myself, Geoffrey, but you. Will you be able to accept this and then bury it from your mind? I can't help what my parents did. I'm only responsible for my own actions, and my actions have been above reproach. For Pete's sake, I haven't even been issued a summons for a moving traffic violation!''

"Keep your voice down, Val, please. Mother will hear.''

"Heaven forbid she learns the truth! If she doesn't approve of me now, what on earth would she say if she knew?'' Val went on, growing more wounded in spirit by the moment. All she wanted him to say was, ''I love you, and I'll stick by your side . . . no matter what.'' Only he didn't.

Valerie flicked a sudden tear from her eye. "Surely your mother must have challenged your wisdom in keeping Corinne, a single mother-to-be, in your office. People would talk. That didn't seem to matter to you then, like this does now. Oh I know, you weren't being considered for Chief of Pediatrics at that time. But if you were, I really wonder if you would have given it a second thought. You're very protective of her, Geoffrey. I've always noticed that about you. It's almost as though you and she are bonded together by a deep dark secret and . . . '' She stopped rambling on as the thought hit her for the first time. "Who was Amanda's father, anyway?''

"In view of the fact that the baby's no longer here, I really don't think it's any of your business.''

"None of my business?'' she repeated incredulously. "And just what am I to draw from that statement? I'm to tell you every hurtful event in my distant past, yet you're expected to keep silent about the recent events in your own life.''

"Valerie, you can't actually believe what you're implying.''

"Then tell me, Geoff. All you have to do is give me a name.''

"If you're really that determined to know, ask Corinne. For now, let's get back on the track and talk about our future."

"Our future? I'm beginning to think we really don't have one! I'll make it easy for you. I'll bow out of your life now, before the story you're so sure is going to break, does." As she spoke, Val twisted the large diamond off her finger and placed it on the mantel.

The distraught young woman hurried upstairs, took her suitcase out of the armoire and opened it across the bed. She'd expected him to chase after her, pleading with her to stay, but he didn't. Tears washed down her cheeks as she began to pack and her hands were shaking badly as she tried to neatly fold her garments.

As she returned to the armoire to retrieve a blouse, she caught her breath in surprise. Geoffrey, who'd slipped in unnoticed, was standing there now, his arms folded across his chest, watching her in deep disappointment. He spoke first in a tone which was neither angry or impatient. "Just what do you think you're doing, Val?"

"What does it look like?" she retorted, uncharacteristically childish.

"It looks to me like you're not thinking very clearly. You're upset and I can understand that, but this is not the time to be making life-changing decisions."

"Please step aside so I can get the rest of my things."

He looked down at her, not knowing whether to take her passionately into his arms and kiss her as he'd never done before or to literally shake her. He did neither. But he did speak in a rather brusque manner. "You are not leaving this house, Val!"

As he expected, that defiant little chin tilted up. "And how do you propose to stop me, Geoff? Lock me in my room?"

"That is an idea. You're letting your emotions override your common sense. And don't give me that look, Val . . . I just hate it when you do that. Honestly, woman, you can be more aggravating at times than Ryan."

"Will you please step aside," she repeated, more determined than ever.

Geoff tossed his hands in the air in a gesture of giving up, then moved away. Arguing with her was getting him absolutely nowhere. Maybe he'd get further by using reverse psychology—a ruse he hadn't tried yet.

"Here," he said, scooping up the toiletries from the dresser and laying them in the suitcase. "Don't forget these. And better make sure you haven't left anything in the bathroom. If there's anything I hate, it's bumping into pantyhose draped over the bar to dry."

"I haven't left any in there." She closed the lid, then turned to face him. She lifted a suspicious brow, but the thoughts swirling about in his head were unreadable. "I'll . . . um . . . phone for a taxi," she said at last.

"No need. I'll drive you back to your apartment and then check around to make sure no one's been inside."

"But no one could have been. Gilbert changed the locks, remember."

He smiled tightly, noticing the informal way she'd referred to Ellis now. Gone was the formal "lieutenant," for his benefit, no doubt. "That might have stopped the stalker from getting in, true. But what are you going to do if he starts calling you every five minutes? And tomorrow, when you leave the apartment to meet with clients, how on earth are you going to concentrate, never knowing if he's watching for the perfect chance to grab you and do whatever it is he's planning to do? Perhaps your anger with me justifies taking such chances." He cocked his head, looking her direct in the eye. "Does it, Val?"

Valerie exhaled deeply as she sank down on the edge of the bed. "Maybe . . . maybe I have been acting in haste."

"Do I take that to mean you're ready to discuss this like two rational people?"

The young woman nodded mutely and he went on. "I'm glad to see your sanity has returned. I really wouldn't have wanted to lock you in or restrain you to a chair, or even drug your bedtime hot chocolate to keep you here."

He saw the anger flash in her eyes for a second and held up his hands in a gesture of surrender. "Just kidding, Val . . . just kidding." Then he extended his hand. "Friends?"

"Friends," she agreed as she slipped hers in his.

He didn't release it, but reached in the pocket of his dress pants, extracted the diamond and slipped it back on. "The next time you pull that off in a fit of anger, I might not be so quick to slip it back on."

"Are you sure you want to now?"

"Not a doubt." His vague smile faded and he became dead serious. "Valerie, we've both been under an inordinate amount of stress lately, but please, let's not turn on each other."

"Were you really going to take me back to my apartment?"

He hesitated before answering. "If I said no, I was only trying to get you to see the folly of what you were doing, would that set you off again?"

"No." She smiled a little helplessly. "I'm sorry, Geoff. I know I haven't been the easiest person to live with lately. I'm usually very even-keeled."

"And you will be again, once this nightmare's behind us." He drew her into his arms and held her. As she laid her head on his chest, she could hear the steady beat of his heart through the softness of his cranberry sweater. And in the quietness of that moment, her thoughts turned to Corinne's deceased baby and his stubborn refusal to answer her question. Why couldn't he be open with her about this matter, which was suddenly beginning to nag her?

Val, you're being hypocritical, a little voice within reminded her. *What about your own feelings toward Gil? If it were he who had his arms wrapped around you, your lips would be pressed to his, not just standing there, staring into space. You keep pressing your feelings down. When are you going to be honest with yourself and with the two men in your life?*

"Leave me alone."

"What?" Geoffrey drew back and looked down at her, perplexed.

Val's cheeks grew crimson, horrified that she'd spoken out loud to her touchy conscience. "I . . . um . . . " she stammered, then lied to spare his feelings. "I was just thinking about Saget and telling him to leave me alone."

"I'm holding you, and you're thinking about Saget?" He looked appropriately hurt, but not as hurt as he would be if he really knew the swirl of thoughts which were floating around in Valerie's troubled mind. "He's the farthest thing from my thoughts, and he should be the last thing in yours too, Val," he gently chided.

"I know, but it's hard to be romantic at a time like this." She shrugged and smiled a little helplessly; he didn't return that smile but looked decisively grim.

"Perhaps a little romance is just what this doctor ordered. You must get your mind on something else besides Saget . . . or is it really someone else, Val?" he asked bluntly. "I keep getting this feeling that Saget's only a smokescreen."

"Be patient with me, Geoff, please."

"I think I have been." His arms slid from her and slipped into his trouser pockets. "Valerie, I hope you won't be foolish enough to toss all this aside. I'm offering you a very enviable life here—a life, if you'll excuse the trite expression, that many women would give their eyeteeth for. I'm not accustomed to being shunned, and once we're married, I won't accept any feeble excuses. I do expect and need you to respond and not stand there like some mannequin, staring into space. End of speech.'' His tone mellowed. ''Shall I help you unpack?''

''Thank you, but it won't take me long.''

Somewhere in the house they could hear the clock chime out twelve times, and Geoffrey said they'd better call it a night. ''I have a busy schedule tomorrow and I did promise Ryan we'd take him to see the Christmas Village in the evening.''

Val lifted a suspicious brow. ''In return for treating me more civilly? I couldn't help but notice he gave me a tentative good-night hug.''

''Give him time, Val, he will come around to accept you.'' Words of optimistic assurance—he always offered her these. Geoffrey walked toward the open door, then turned and looked back at the woman who looked so dejected, standing there in the middle of the room. ''Do you think you'll be able to sleep?''

Her answer was an honest one. ''I'm not sure.''

''I can give you something to help you relax.''

''I don't want anything. I'll be fine, really. I'll . . . um . . . count sheep if need be,'' she finished lamely.

Geoff hesitated a moment, considering her circumstance. ''Would you agree to seeing Doctor Westlake?''

A faint frown gathered on her brow. ''He's a psychiatrist. Do you really think I need one?''

''I think you need to talk out your feelings, Val.''

''I am dealing with my past.''

''No, you're not . . . your past is dealing with you.'' She opened her mouth to protest, but he was quick to cut her off. "Let's not start up again. Look, if you won't agree to work it through with Westlake, will you at least do some reading on the subject? I have a book written for the layman and it can help get you in touch with your emotions and to quit stuffing them down as you've been so prone to do. Will you accept it?"

How could she say no, she wondered, so Valerie nodded. A few minutes later it was in her hands and Geoffrey headed back to his room.

As Geoff stepped out of his trousers and reached for his pajamas, his eyes lifted to the oil painting of the auburn-haired beauty over his bed. His throat tightened unexpectedly as he remembered her vibrant smile, the quick sparkle in her eyes and her bubbly laughter when he held her in his arms. "Oh Jessie, I miss you so much. Why did you have to leave us this soon," he murmured.

Valerie reminded him of Jessica in looks. That he felt was what had made him divert his interest from Alexandra and focus it on her. If only there weren't this real or imagined entanglement with Ellis. She couldn't have any deep feelings for this guy, could she? he wondered. The thought needled him. Like an annoying splinter under the skin, he was ever conscious of its presence.

Drawing the covers back, he slid beneath the quilt of the comfortable, antique bed. It was a find of Jessie's which she fell in love with during a treasure-seeking trip through Vermont. She'd told him it wouldn't be going in her shop, but in their room. Here they shared the joy of conceiving Ryan, and here he experienced the heartbreak of waking up to find himself a widower.

Geoffrey rolled over and reached out to touch the empty space Jessica had left. Could Valerie fill this aching, empty void in his life? For the first time since he set his designs on having her, he was beginning to wonder.

The very nature of his thoughts jarred him. Of course he wasn't making a mistake. It had been an eventful day—an eventful couple of days, actually, and stress was beginning to take its toll on them both. He would wake up tomorrow refreshed and upbeat, ready to face the challenges of a new day. Convinced of this, he closed his eyes and quickly drifted off to sleep.

Valerie skimmed through the book, reading a paragraph here and there, but she couldn't concentrate. After several minutes, she gave up and laid it aside. She was too distracted to bring her wandering thoughts into captivity. What on earth was the matter with her? Geoffrey's words were not the words of an egotist—they were spoken in simple truth. Many women *would* have given their eyeteeth to be his wife. A woman could wait a lifetime for someone like Geoff to come along. He was the perfect man . . . incredibly hand-some . . . engaged in a promising career . . . and he truly was family-oriented. Now, what more could she ask?

"Oh Gil, why did you choose now to come back?" she said aloud, deeply frustrated. If she could just hang on till the twenty-fourth, she would be Mrs. Geoffrey Faraday. That is, if Gil didn't somehow break her fragile resolve, or worse yet, the stalker terminate her very life.

Val drew the covers back and switched off the light, but she didn't crawl between the body-warmed covers. Instead, she walked over to the window and opened the drapes. The young woman glanced across the moonlit landscape. She could see the outline of the ruins now that she knew where they existed. Or was that just a trick of her imagination?

As Val's attention focused on the edge of the property, she reached out and pressed her palm against the cold pane. Had Jessica been standing at this very window that night, perhaps searching the clear sky for signs of that mythical flying sleigh? Had she been the first to see the flames leap out the windows of the Saget house and alert her grandfather? And he, bless his heart, had pulled her from Karl's clutches.

A tear rolled down her cheek as her thoughts turned to her father. "Oh Daddy," she whispered, "if you could have looked down the corridor of time, would you have conducted yourself differently? After all these years, I'm still paying and I wonder where it will end."

Chapter 10

Valerie walked over to the ruins and surveyed them with different eyes than she had yesterday. This is where it all happened. Could she ever be truly happy here? Could she? Val wasn't sure. She would talk to Geoffrey about bringing the walls down and clearing the land. It could be landscaped so that all traces of the old farmhouse would be eradicated.

The young woman went to the gaping opening where the door had once been. As she stood there, her hand resting on the side of the crumbling wall, she forced herself to come to terms with the tragedy in her past.

In her childhood perspective, Patrick Quinn was the most wonderful man who ever walked the face of the earth. He was a big guy, with red hair and a bushy mustache that tickled when he kissed her. He had a gift of making her laugh after her mother made her cry. He'd bought her a doll that Christmas, but stressed it was to be their secret, for her mother had insisted such things were a waste of money. He suggested they keep the doll concealed in an old grocery bag behind the front seat of his vehicle. Val called her Shannon; she had red hair like herself and her father. Her father hadn't said much as he drove to the Saget house, but the one thing he did say, she remembered. He said he knew life was hard with her mother, but all that was about to change. And it did—however, not the way he'd intended.

Val recalled her father leading her into the old-fashioned kitchen, her precious dollie cradled in one arm and the other tucked through his red and black Woolrich. She could remember it as clearly as though it were yesterday.

"Buddy, this is Kaylene," he'd said by way of introduction, "but I call her Katie. I think it's time you two get to know each other. She's my pride and joy, so you be nice to her, son."

And for awhile he was. As she thought back over it, it seemed a curious statement to make, as though there was some question in his mind that he wouldn't be. The young boy had offered her some home-baked doughnuts and a tall glass of raw milk, fresh from that morning's milking.

Val could still visualize Mrs. Saget in her large, humble kitchen. Though rather frail-looking, she was pretty, but the thing that impressed her most about this woman was her friendliness. Buddy's mother said she was so glad to finally meet her, then gave the child a hug and a kiss on the cheek. A feeling of cozy warmth spread through Val, and when her eyes met her father's, he was beaming with approval. Valerie was so starved for maternal affection that she took an instant liking to the lady with golden hair and blue eyes. Then the children were left alone to eat their snacks and get acquainted.

A third adult joined the two in the front room a few minutes later. The children could hear the trio's voices rise

in sudden anger. Not long after that, her father came back
into the kitchen and ordered her to go out to the truck, while
Buddy was sent to his room. She didn't know what really
happened after that. No one did—all was pure conjecture.
Had she disobeyed and stayed, no telling what she would
have witnessed.

A twig behind her snapped, pulling her out of her reverie.
Val's initial image of a deer was quickly dispelled when a
voice called out, ''Katie? Katie Quinn?''

Val forced herself to turn, and standing there was a man
in a navy parka and a trim blond beard. The landscape tilted
at a crazy angle. She couldn't faint and be at his mercy.
Not now!

He took his hands from his pockets and stretched them
out imploringly. ''Katie, I had to see you face to face. I'm
Karl Saget.''

Valerie emitted a pathetic little ''Oh!'' watching him take
a step toward her. And somehow, she managed to make her
shaky legs run toward the house. She could see the rambling
estate break through the trees, but when she reached the
snow-patched lawn, he'd caught up with her. Firm fingers
closed around her upper arm and he spun her around. Time
ran together and suddenly it was twenty years ago. She
opened her mouth to scream, but nothing came out but a
strangled gasp. *See me, Monica*, she pleaded silently, her
wild eyes turning longingly toward the house. *Look out the
window and see me!*

But why would she? Valerie had told Geoff's mother that
she was going to her room to read. No one knew she was
out of the house or they wouldn't have let her go alone.
Everything was working against her, even her own vocal
cords, paralyzed with such fear she couldn't even let out
one healthy scream. But she did beat at his chest with her
clenched fists.

"Katie! Katie, stop it!" he commanded. "Cut it out now!"

He released his grip enough that she could break free, and once again, she was racing blindly toward the house. After a moment's hesitation, Karl began chasing after her. The blast of a horn and the screeching of tires brought them both to a halt. Valerie whirled around, expecting to see Geoffrey. What she saw was even better and it triggered tears of relief.

One look at Gil's angry face said it all. Alighting quickly, he slammed the door shut, then demanded, "Karl! What in the name of common sense do you think you're doing?"

The man spread his arms rather helplessly. "I had to see her."

Valerie fled to Gil, where he gave her the reassuring hug she'd so badly needed just then. But his eyes remained on Saget. "Come on, let's all go inside where we can talk."

Val lifted a pair of uncertain eyes to her rescuer. "Aren't you going to cuff him and read him his rights, or whatever it is you guys do?" she asked, her voice not failing her now.

"No." He shook his head, still not able to believe it. "It's a good thing I drove by when I did and saw your van pulled into that weed-choked lane, Saget. It beats the fire out of me that you would even consider trying such a stupid stunt."

"I didn't mean any harm, honest."

"I know you didn't," Gil wearily conceded, then gestured for them to move toward the door.

The trio entered the foyer, to be confronted by a freckle-faced dynamo in a cowboy hat. Gil drew in his breath, startled, as the suction-tipped projectile smacked him in the backside.

"Ryan!" Valerie scolded, spinning around.

"Uh-oh!" he exclaimed, his lips forming a perfect *O* as he realized what he had done.

Monica came around the corner at that point, cheeks flushed, realizing by Val's outcry that Ryan was up to his antics again. The young woman's gaze shifted from the youngster to the grandmother and she made the necessary introductions.

Monica's eyes lingered on Gil. Though the name Saget had little meaning to her, the name Ellis did and her lips pressed in a thin line of disapproval. Geoffrey had spoken of him a few times lately and always in a negative way. Ryan's eyes were fastened on Gil, too, only his were wide with wonder.

"Are you a real cop?"

"That's right, partner." Gilbert stooped to get eye-level with him. "Are you a real cowboy?"

Ryan giggled, finding that question so silly, it didn't require an answer. Then he sobered, his gaze coming to rest on Gil's revolver. "Did you ever shoot a bad guy?"

"No, and I hope I'm never forced to. It's no fun getting shot, not even with this," Gil said, pointing to the toy gun.

The child put the plaything to his side. "Are you after the man who's after Val?"

Gil nodded. "You know anything about it, son?"

The child went on, feeling a sense of importance that he was included in such a conversation. "My dad said she was shot, and it's making her nervous. That's why she yells at me a lot."

Valerie's cheeks reddened, but it was Monica who spoke his name reprovingly. "He did tell me that, Grandma," Ryan insisted, looking up at her. "And he said we should be extra nice to her right now."

"We must always be nice to people, Ryan," the flustered

woman said. "Let's not waste anymore of the lieutenant's time. I'm sure he has things to discuss with Val."

"You catch 'im, officer," the little boy said, "so Val don't got to be scared no more."

"I will, partner," Gil said, then his voice dropped a bit as he spoke man-to-man with the child who was obviously so much in awe of him. "If you see anyone suspicious hanging around Stoneybrook, you tell your grandma or dad so they can call me."

The boy's eyes shifted questioningly to the grim, silent stranger beside Gil and the policeman was quick to assure him that this man was okay. Then he went on, "Another thing, son, don't go around shooting that thing at folks anymore. Deal?" Gilbert held out his hand and the boy shook it soberly. Only then was Ryan ready to allow his grandmother to escort him from the room. But as they left, he stole one last look over his shoulder in wide-eyed wonder and Gil heard him say as they rounded the corner, "Grandmom, when I get big, I wanna be a cop too and chase after bad men."

Gilbert straightened up and his smile faded; he became all business. "Will you take us some place where we can talk privately?"

Valerie led them to the great room and there they all seated themselves on the sofa, with Gil in the center as mediator. Val positioned herself at an angle so she could see her childhood nemesis. Now he didn't appear to be such a monster, and the eyes which stared back at her were not cold and menacing, but decidedly sympathetic. Then Val peered at hands faintly burn-scarred, but he began to speak, drawing her attention back to his face.

"I'm sorry I frightened you, Katie. My intentions, believe me, were quite the opposite."

"Let's understand something here," Gil cut in as he

unzipped his jacket and laid it behind him. "The lady's name is Valerie. She chose to use her middle name after the house burned down in an effort to separate herself from the past."

"I can understand that," Karl assured him.

Valerie folded her hands over her crossed knees and came right to the point. "Did you fire that shot at me on Friday night or harass me with those awful phone calls over the weekend?"

"No, I did not," he replied, looking her straight in the eye. "I knew nothing about this until Lieutenant Ellis showed up at my door last night. You must believe that."

Val's gaze shifted to Gil. "Does he have an alibi for Friday evening?"

"Yes, and a solid one at that. Karl's a guidance counselor and he was in a meeting with the parents of one of the students at the school where he works. On Saturday, at the time you were receiving those calls, he was hosting an eighth birthday party for his son. According to his helper, Karl never left the room to use the phone. Sunday night, when you received the last call, he was in bed, asleep. His wife can vouch for that; she was lying right beside him, reading."

"So, there's no shadow of a doubt in your mind?"

"None whatsoever."

The man in question leaned forward, his elbows on his knees. "Katie's not the only victim here." He smiled apologetically. "Excuse me . . . Valerie. I'm a victim too. I've worked very hard to get where I am today. If anyone brought this out in the open, that I was accused of shooting you, then tormenting you with those devilish tapes, I could very well lose my job. I've got a wife and three kids. They're why I had to come to see you . . . to straighten out this mess, at least my innocence in it. I'm not your adversary. I've convinced Lieutenant Ellis of that, I wish I could convince you of that as well.''

Val reflected a moment. "Do you drive a pickup?"

"No. I own a minivan; my wife operates a red Dodge. I understand your stalker was in a truck."

She nodded glumly, then queried, "Why were you at the ruins? And how did you know that I'd be there?"

"I didn't. I hadn't been back since the night of the fire. I don't know, maybe it was morbid curiosity, but suddenly I felt I had to return, to see if it really was over, or if some of the old ghosts which used to haunt my dreams were still around."

"Are they?"

"No."

She stared at him for a moment before speaking. "They are for me. That night you said you'd get me someday."

"I said a lot of things I didn't mean. I had good reason to think your father started that fire. I was out of my head with grief when you last saw me, and for several years after, I was one mixed-up kid. Then one day, a guidance counselor got his hands on me and set me straight. His unwavering attention generated an interest in me to go into that field." He smiled approvingly at her. "From what I hear, you haven't done so badly yourself."

"Some would say so, but it's been an uphill battle, and now not being able to work for who knows how long is really going to set me back."

"You hang in there, Valerie, and if there's anything I can do to help, anything at all, you just let me know."

"Thanks, but you've already done more than you realize. I've lived in fear of you since this nightmare began. Now I see those fears were totally unfounded."

"Your fear of me, yes, but someone out there is after you."

Val rose and walked over to the fireplace; she stared sadly down at the ashes. "If he calls again, I swear, I don't know how I'll handle it."

Karl came up behind her and gave her shoulder an encouraging pat. "Sooner or later he'll do something stupid and then Lieutenant Ellis will nab him. Oh, before I forget, I have something I want to give you." Reaching in his pocket, he withdrew a sealed envelope and handed it to her. "I looked up your address in the phone book this morning and was going to mail this to you. Now I don't have to."

Valerie accepted it, puzzled. "What is it?"

"Read it when you have the time to give it your full attention. I'm sure it will answer some haunting questions. When your stalker's caught, I'd like you to give me a call. My name's in the Reading phone book." He smiled sheepishly. "That's how the lieutenant found me so quickly. And you know, I'm glad I wasn't the guy he was after. As intense as he seems to feel about you, I think he would have forgotten he was sworn to uphold the law, not break it," he finished with a wink. Then he looked back at Gil, who was now rising to his feet. "Mind if I leave? I promised the kids I'd take them to the mall to see Santa. My youngest still believes."

The lawman nodded. Karl started for the door, then turned and gave the room one final look before his eyes met Valerie's once more. "t seems it was another lifetime that I was here, in this house. The Simmons were such nice folks. I understand they're dead now too. Almost everyone connected with that night is, except us."

"It seems that way. Good night, Karl, and thank you," Val murmured, shoving the envelope in her pocket. She watched him disappear out of the room before turning a pair of weary eyes to the advancing officer. "So, we're back to square one. Again."

Gil reached out and brushed away the sudden tear that was rolling down her cheek. "Don't. Don't cry, Val. I'll get this guy, I swear I will."

"How? You don't even know who he is or why he's doing this."

Gilbert stood in reflective silence for a moment. "Maybe that's because you're not the real source of his twisted hatred. Maybe you're a pawn in some sinister game."

"What do you mean, pawn?"

"Perhaps Faraday's the actual target. Yes . . . could be someone is getting back at him by getting to you," he said, thinking it out aloud. "It wouldn't take much detective work to check those old newspaper articles in the library once he understood that you were involved. Val, are you certain that someone doesn't have it in for Faraday? If a parent lost their child because of something the doc did or didn't do, could be he feels justified in striking back at someone close to the doc—namely you."

"No, Gil," Val disagreed, not seeing it that way. "Geoffrey's an exceptional doctor. He's very thorough and competent. He loves kids. I see that all the time in his rapport with Megan, who simply idolizes the man."

"I'm not disputing he's good with kids. Maybe the patient was beyond help, but the father doesn't see it that way. Has he lost any children recently?"

"I don't know. Geoff doesn't talk much about his work. When he's with me, he puts that part of his life behind."

"Can't say that I blame him there. When I'm around you, the last thing I want to think about is my latest arrest. However, this is a rare exception." He smiled glumly, then persisted. "Are you sure Faraday hasn't said anything disturbing about his practice, no matter how insignificant? What about an abusive parent he might have blown the whistle on?"

"I think you're getting yourself further and further off track here."

"There's got to be some logical explanation and it's probably glaring me right in the face. I'm just too blind to see it."

"You're just too close to your subject."

"I won't argue there." Gil heaved a heavy sigh and decided it was time to put it from his mind, at least for a little while. His eyes shifted from her to the mantel and the photograph of the man and woman standing by the pool. "Who's the couple?"

"Jessica, Geoffrey's first wife, and her brother, Adrian."

He studied the picture for a moment. "She's a striking woman, Val. You resemble her. Think that might have occurred to your baby doctor boyfriend as well?"

"Cut it out, Gil. I'm not in any mood for your verbal jabs."

"Did you ever meet this Adrian?"

"No. I don't think Geoff's been very close to him. He never had much to say about him, not even when I asked him about the photo. He simply told me who he was, then continued on with the tour of the house. He's never mentioned him since."

"That's interesting."

"But not suspicious. Not everyone gets along well with their in-laws." She turned the subject back to the matter that weighed so heavily upon her. "Where do we go from here, Gil?"

"I don't know," he said truthfully. "I'm as disappointed as you are about the way things have turned out, believe me. I was leaning on this Saget to be the one."

When he looked into Val's sad, dejected face, which revealed so clearly the torment within, he was unable to keep his feelings distant any longer. Reaching out, he wrapped his arms about her and drew her against him. She didn't resist his comfort and affection, and realizing this gave him added confidence. "I love you, Valerie. You were the special first love of my life and now, after all these years, I still can't get you out of my mind. I suppose I never will."

"Me too," she confessed, laying her head against his chest. "But it's too late for us."

"Why? Engagements can be broken." He glanced around the room he found himself in and shook his head. "But then, why would you want to? I must be pretty dense to think you'd ever consider giving this all up to be my wife in that handyman's special. You know I wouldn't have bought it had I not thought there was a good chance of you living in it with me someday."

"This kind of talk is futile and it's wrong. My life is forged with Geoffrey's."

"Has he ever told you he loved you?"

"Not in so many words, but then, not many men feel comfortable verbalizing their feelings like you do."

"You need to hear it, Val, often. It's the last thing you'd hear before you'd fall asleep in my arms at night. I'd do my best to make up for all those years that you felt unwanted and unloved. You'd never feel lonely again, I swear it." He ran a caressing finger across her cheek. "Val, look at me. You're not the only one who needs to hear they're loved and cherished. I need to hear it too. Tell me, darling. It's very hard for me to believe you don't when you're letting me hold you like this."

Val watched his head bend toward hers and she was powerless to move. She wanted to feel his kisses. What on earth was wrong with her! She wasn't a schoolgirl experiencing her first romantic encounter. "Gil, don't," she whispered, but she knew he didn't want to hear her feeble pleas.

With his hand stroking her back and his eyes focused on her lips, he was oblivious to everything save her.

"Tell me it's me you love and not your baby doctor," he urged.

At that moment Val caught a movement from the corner of her eye. Monica Faraday came into the room and stopped dead in her tracks. Val gasped, and Gil turned, his hand still on her.

Of all times! Val thought miserably. *That woman has no sense of timing.*

With cheeks flushed deeply, Monica was the first to find her voice. "Geoffrey's on the phone, or shall I tell him you're indisposed right now?"

"No, I'll take it," she replied and walked out of the room with as much dignity as she could muster. Going to the den, she closed the door so she could speak in private. Val took a deep breath and with a hand that was still shaking, she lifted the receiver to her ear. "Hello, Geoff."

"Val, I just called to let you know I'm sending Corie over to get you in a few minutes. I phoned the garage and they said your car's ready. I know you've been feeling cooped up, so I thought you might as well have some limited freedom as soon as possible. I have to insist on one condition, however, and that's that you don't go anywhere alone. Corie will follow you back to Stoneybrook to make sure you arrive safely."

"Are you sure you can spare her that long?"

"Better than I can one of my nurses." He sighed deeply, his thoughts jumping to another subject. "I hope this Saget's soon found so we can resume a normal life."

Val twisted the cord nervously around her fingers. "Geoff, Lieutenant Ellis came to . . ." She broke off, hearing voices in the background.

A moment later he turned his attention back to her. "Got

to run, Val. A child's just been brought in with a badly lacerated knee. Oh, and don't forget tonight we'll be going to the Christmas Village. I offered to take Megan along; hope you don't mind. See you later, dear.''

She managed to say her own good-bye at the same time she heard the receiver click. Of course she didn't mind that he was taking Megan along, although she wished he would have consulted her before offering.

When Valerie returned to the great room, she found Monica sitting on the wing chair by the hearth. "He left," Monica informed the young woman, noticing her eyes sweeping across the area. "Your friend received a call and had to leave abruptly—police business. He said he hoped you'd understand." *But I don't*, her expression said.

Val knew Monica couldn't have heard their whispered conversation, but she surely saw their stance—much too intimate to be purely business. However, Monica was too prideful to ask the questions really bombarding her mind at that point. And Valerie was bent on avoiding the conversation that would open the door to invite Monica to ask. She sufficed to say that Corie was on her way, and with that left the tension-filled room to get ready.

Corie didn't follow Val directly back to Stoneybrook, but to Val's apartment. Val checked her mail, poured some expired milk down the drain, and threw out a half loaf of stale bread. Lastly, she sat on the sofa beside the receptionist and played her recorded telephone messages. Four were from clients. These she jotted down and slipped the numbers into her handbag to call at her leisure back at the estate.

"At least your stalker didn't leave any more messages. Maybe he's decided to call it quits," Corie suggested.

"He never leaves a message. I'm sure he doesn't want

that kind of evidence falling into the hands of the authorities.''

''Have the police found that Saget character yet?''

''Yes,'' Val admitted, none too enthusiastically. ''He came out to the house to see me today. It's not him, Corie. There's not a shadow of a doubt about that, and I don't mind telling you, I wish it had been. Now Gil doesn't have a clue who it is he's after.''

Corie was thoughtfully quiet for a moment. ''Maybe I do.''

''What?'' Val looked at her curiously. ''What do you know about this, Corie?''

The receptionist rose, walked to the window, and peered out between the lifted slats of the blinds. When she turned around after a moment, Valerie thought she appeared at war with her conscience. The young woman slid forward. ''Corinne, if you know something, no matter how insignificant it might seem to you, you must tell me. Please. It's my life we're talking about here.''

Corie returned to the sofa, folded her arms across her plain white blouse, and weighed her words carefully. ''Has Geoff ever spoken to you about Adrian?''

''Not other than to tell me he was his brother-in-law.''

''It doesn't surprise me that he's pretty quiet where Adrian's concerned. They didn't get along. Adrian was terribly jealous of Geoff. He felt he'd gotten a raw deal and I suppose, in a way, he did.''

Val leaned forward but resisted the temptation to prod Corie. It was obvious it was hard for her to talk about it. Was it out of loyalty to Geoff? After all, had he wanted her to know about his wife's brother, he would have told her.

''Adrian has a problem,'' Corie explained, still not very sure. ''He drinks a lot and then he says and does things he's later sorry for. Oh, Valerie, he can't afford any more disappointments in life and I'm afraid if this gets out, your officer friend will twist it to make an arrest and he'll lose his business. That's all he has anymore.''

"Gil's not like that, Corie. He doesn't go around arresting someone unless he has a darn good reason, nor does he nab them to close a case—guilty or not. What sense would that make if the real criminal were still free?'' Val looked at her intently. "Now, what did Adrian do that makes you suspect he might be involved in this? You said he was jealous.''

"Yes. He, as the only grandson, counted on inheriting Stoneybrook, but Mr. Simmons left everything to Jessie. He said Adrian was as irresponsible as his father, and between his excessive drinking and gambling, he would lose the estate to loan sharks in no time. So level-headed, business-minded Jessie inherited the whole kit and caboodle. Naturally Adrian was upset, being totally cut out. When she married Geoff, Geoff automatically came on Adrian's hate list and Adrian let his feelings be known right from the start. He'd crash parties and do a host of other things to humiliate Geoff.''

"Didn't Geoff ever seek legal advice or get a restraining order?''

"No. It was a family matter and Geoff wanted to keep it private. He tried to get Adrian into a clinic to dry out, but to no avail. And Jessie, in spite of it all, loved and pitied her brother. I think Geoff remained so patient in the midst of all the chaos Adrian created for her sake. Then when she died so suddenly and he showed up before the funeral drunk, he really outdid himself. Adrian actually accused Geoff of doing something to cause his sister's death so Stoneybrook would be entirely his. He said Geoffrey only married Jessie for her money, but he said the plan wouldn't work. He claimed the estate could never mean as much to Geoff as it did to him and he'd get it back someday or . . . or ruin Geoff.'' She shook her head. ''Alex and I were there—we saw the whole sorry incident. Geoff was furious. He gave Adrian the choice of admitting himself to the hospital to detoxify or he was going to have him arrested for harassment and defamation. Apparently prison scared him more than the hospital because he agreed to go.''

''Has he remained sober?''

''I don't know, Val. To my knowledge he hasn't come around Stoneybrook since. He'd better have shaped up. He owns a garage. He does inspection and body work—that sort of thing. But if he is on the wagon and has been behaving himself, and accusations are made that he is your stalker, this could destroy not only his business but him as well.''

''But if it is Adrian, Corie, he can't be allowed to get away with this. I have to tell Gil what you've just related to me.''

''I'm sure it isn't Adrian.''

But as Val dialed the station, she was sure that it was. The other child in the Simmon's house twenty years ago, that boy, she now knew had to have been Jessie's brother Adrian. That was what was disturbing about the pictures. Those eyes were as mistrusting and hard in the recent photograph as they were twenty years ago. Aside from Karl, Adrian was the only other living person who would have remembered her as Katie, and the details of the tragedy that struck them that night.

Gil was right. She was the pawn in this war on nerves.

Chapter 11

Visiting the Christmas Village was the last thing Valerie was in the mood to do, but for the children's sake, she kept up a cheerful front. Val held Megan's hand as they walked among the colorful exhibits, and the little girl's face was animated with the innocent joy of childhood. They walked down the lighted walkways, exclaiming over the exhibits and the familiar carols that accompanied them. Ryan was especially intrigued with the train platform, which featured several separate train systems running at the same time. He followed the train through the tunnel, across the high trestle, and around the miniature village. His face beamed as he looked at his father and said he'd like one just like it.

Geoffrey laughed as he ran a playful hand through the boy's hair. If it had been within his power, Val knew he would have bought the whole train assembly.

On the way home, they stopped for dessert at a restaurant. Ryan ordered a banana split, daring Val to contradict his wish. She didn't. As she leisurely ate her own sundae, Megan said wistfully that she wished Geoffrey could be her daddy. He explained that while he loved her with a very special love, he could never be that. She thought this over a moment and said, then when she grew up, she wanted to be his nurse. He told her he thought that was a very workable idea.

As Ryan looked up, he dripped chocolate syrup on his clean pants. He put in his two cents that when he was big, he wanted to be a cop and hunt for bad guys, just like the one who visited them today. From the sudden change in Geoffrey's expression, Val knew that was one idea he didn't think much of. But before he could pick up on the subject, the waitress returned with the tab, and with a smile, told Geoff what a nice-looking family he had. He didn't take the time to correct her, but only murmured a polite "thank you."

By the time they arrived in town, both children were asleep in the back seat. Megan never awoke when Geoff carried her into the apartment and placed her in bed. Val thought he had been exceptionally quiet ever since they left the restaurant. She didn't know whether he too was tired or something was weighing heavily on his mind. She found out it was the latter when he joined her in the kitchen. Valerie was sitting at the table, foregoing her usual hot chocolate for a sleep-promoting glass of warm milk.

"We have to talk, Val," he said, his tone very serious.

We certainly do, she thought regretfully. Val had been wanting to tell Geoff about Adrian, but didn't have him alone long enough to do it—until now. Her lips parted to speak at the same time he began.

"Mother told me about Karl Saget's uninvited visit this afternoon."

Just how much did she tell you? Val wondered as she set

her glass down. From the look on his face, she had a pretty good idea. All right, looks like she would deal with Karl and Gil before confronting him about Adrian.

"Karl scared the life out of me, showing up the way he did, but he's not the one, Geoff. I was so frustrated after he left, I felt we were right back at zero again." She offered him a weak smile, hoping he'd understand the situation. "I was so close to tears. I guess that's why Gil put his arms around me, to comfort me. I imagine your mother couldn't wait to tell you what she saw after walking in on the scene."

Geoffrey placed his palms down on the table and leaned forward, seemingly weighing his words before he spoke them. His eyes never left hers and she saw a potpourri of emotions there, but the overriding one seemed to be deep hurt. "Valerie, Mother never told me a thing about Ellis other than that he was here at the house with Saget. This is the first I'm hearing about Ellis hugging you."

Val slumped back in her chair. She'd been too quick to react. When would she ever learn to keep her mouth shut! "You've been so quiet for the past hour. I assumed Lieutenant Ellis was the cause."

"He was, but for an entirely different reason. I don't like my son being so taken with the man. But Ryan's the least of my worries when it appears my fiancée still is. I want him off the case, Val. He's getting absolutely nowhere. He has nothing to go on."

"He does now," she said rising. "Geoffrey, why didn't you tell me about Adrian?"

He seemed to flinch; she'd touched a sore spot. "What about Adrian?"

"Corinne told me how he threatened to get back at you, that he was jealous and resentful."

"Corie had no right to tell you that."

"You don't think I have a right to know? Don't take her

to task for it; she didn't want to tell me. But after I'd explained how we'd run into a dead end with Karl Saget, she felt I should know about Adrian. I should know for my own safety, which makes me think she's more concerned than you are.''

"That's not true.''

Valerie walked over to the counter, then turned to face him once more. "You know, if this weren't so serious, it would almost be funny. All along you were so afraid it was my father's past that would ruin your chances for getting that coveted position, when all along, it might turn out to be a member of your own family . . . your brother-in-law.''

Geoffrey followed her, knowing her frustration and feeling it too. "Adrian's impulsive, yes. He acts without thinking and his drinking certainly exacerbates the problem, but Val, I really can't believe he'd stoop so low as to do anything this despicable. My gosh, he doesn't even know you.''

"Oh, but he does, Geoffrey. Both he and Jessie were here, at Stoneybrook the night of the fire. He remembers me as Katie Quinn. And he remembers Karl Saget. Mr. Simmons tried to quiet him until help arrived, but Karl was hysterical and said a lot of crazy things.'' She folded her arms across her chest and continued to look up into his face, more determined than ever to prove her point. "Alexandra gave our engagement a nice write-up in the newspaper. Adrian must have seen it and all his old hatreds and insecurities were rekindled.''

"Pure conjecture,'' he said, although he did look doubtful and Val knew, even if he weren't ready to admit it yet, Geoff was having serious doubts about what his former in-law was capable of doing. The story he related was pretty much the same as the one Corie had. And when he was finished, he reached out and placed his hands solidly on her shoulders. "Are you certain beyond any possibility of a doubt that it wasn't Saget?"

"Absolutely positive. He's got an iron-clad alibi. And Geoff, even though I was fighting it, I found myself liking the guy. He's involved in school counseling, and he appears to be a man who genuinely loves his work and his family. He wouldn't do anything to jeopardize his position. He said he wanted to meet me and put my mind at ease and clear up his involvement in the case."

"I see." His hands slid from her shoulders to find their way into his pockets. He seemed to have trouble finding the words. "Val, if what you suspect is true, and it turns out to be my brother-in-law who is striking at you to get to me, I don't know how I'll ever make it up to you."

"All I ask is that you be totally open with me in the future."

He nodded mutely, then went on. "It's late and I have a full work load tomorrow. Maybe you and Mother can do some last-minute shopping. You two haven't spent much time together and I'd like you to become friends. It means a lot to me, Valerie."

"I know it does, but I can't do it alone, Geoff. I can't force her to like me."

"Just be yourself and she can't help but like you. I don't know whether to compliment her or be angry with her for not telling me about Ellis. I think she had a right to, but I don't think she wanted to come between us."

A couple of minutes later, they said their good night. Val expected him to take the single step forward to give her that parting kiss, but he didn't. His handsome face bore silent testament to deep concern, not romance, and when he walked out of the kitchen, Val thought he looked as though the weight of the world was bearing down on his shoulders.

After a quick shower, Geoffrey reached for a towel from off the towel warmer, and his eyes lifted to the image in the mirror before him. A few streaks of gray were becoming evident at his temple area . . . marks of distinction, people said. He felt tired, mentally as well as emotionally. He was still grieving over his loss of Jessie, and at times felt an unreasonable guilt for even desiring another woman. Then there was the death of his good friend, John. He'd seen him wince with chest pain when he'd climbed out of the family pool. Why didn't he convince him to have an EKG, or at least a thorough physical. And the baby. How he grieved right along with Corie over that. Now Valerie hit him with this bombshell. How much more could his life be shattered?

Geoffrey slipped into his black velour robe. He wished she'd be totally honest with him about her feelings toward Gil. But how could he expect her to be honest when he couldn't be truthful enough to tell her who the father of Corie's baby had been when she asked? What difference did it make now? But too quickly, he had promised Corie it would be their secret. *Oh what a tangled web we weave*, he thought miserably.

Geoff went back to his room, drew down the quilt and slipped inside the blue cool sheets. He didn't close his eyes though. Folding his arms behind his head, he stared up at the moonlit ceiling, thinking how little control he really had over the affairs of his own life. Outwardly he was the epitome of success, the envy of his peers—the man who had it all. He smiled bitterly. . . . How little they knew!

When Valerie entered her room, she went directly to the slacks she had folded neatly on the seat of the rocker and slipped her hand into the deep pocket for the letter. Then, lying across the bed, she began to read it. The envelope, though having her proper street address, was simply addressed to Miss Quinn. The letter was neatly typed out on plain white paper.

Dear Kaylene:

I understand that you no longer go by that name, but bear with me, for this is how I remember you. I know hearing from me after all these years is coming as a shock. However, I felt compelled to write.

A Lieutenant Ellis was here this evening, questioning me about events which I had absolutely nothing to do with. I think I've convinced him of my innocence; anyway, I hope I have. Ever since he left, I've done nothing but think about that terrible night, twenty years ago.

I'm sure I said a lot of crazy things then. I can't remember them, though it's obvious you do. I never intended to hurt you, Katie, and I'm thankful that the Simmons's were around to prevent me from doing something really stupid to either of us. You were very young, so I suppose you weren't aware of what was going on in our parent's lives. Mom told me your father was filing for a quick divorce so he could marry her right away. His intention was to bring you to live here with us, but as it turned out, they never had a chance to carry through with their plans. It was assumed by the authorities, though never actually proven, that your father started the deadly blaze.

Aunt Eugenia was the only witness. She knew the truth but kept silent until her con-

science prompted her to speak out on her deathbed. My aunt was terribly jealous of her younger sister, and at some point actually grew to hate her. It wasn't until that night that Aunt Eugenia found out Mom was going to have a baby and she flew into a rage. That was the arguing you and I heard in the kitchen just before you were sent out to the truck and I to my room. My aunt threw a paperweight at Mom and hit her on the head, knocking her out. It seems when she fell, she bumped the table, knocking the kerosene lamp over. The flames quickly ignited the Christmas tree and the curtains beside it. Your father tried to bat it out, but he was overcome by smoke in the process. About then, I came downstairs and saw the three of them lying there. Aware of Mom's condition, I assumed your father was responsible and my aunt never corrected me. After that, I don't remember very much.

I thought you should know this, Katie. Aunt Eugenia only died last year and with such a long passing of time, I felt it would cause more hurt than good, dredging up old feelings, if I went to the authorities with this. The case had been closed years ago. I see now that I was wrong.

I hope this letter puts your mind at ease, knowing your father was not guilty of arson. Mom was lonely and your dad was suffering through a bad marriage. That's not to excuse what they did, but remember this—our parents loved us and had planned their future

*to include you and me, not desert us in their
own passion.*

*I've enclosed my address and phone num-
ber if you should want to contact me. If you
desire to let it go with this, I'll understand.
It's too bad I couldn't have gotten to be your
big brother. I think we would have liked each
other.*

*Best regards,
Karl Saget*

Valerie read and reread the letter several times, letting
the healing words sink in. Her father wasn't guilty of arson
. . . he actually wasn't guilty. Tears of relief washed down
her face as she rolled over on her side and muffled her cries
of relief into the pillow. A twenty-year-old burden had been
lifted—the stigma was gone.

Valerie slept late the next morning. When she came down
for breakfast, she found that Geoffrey had already left for
the office. It was disappointing, for she had wanted to share
her good news with him. It seemed the only time they could
talk was in the evening when the tensions were running high
from the abnormal stresses of the day.

As the afternoon wore on, Val had a growing desire to
go to her father's grave, even though she knew this would
be going against Geoffrey's wishes unless someone accompanied her. But this was a private moment which she didn't
want to share with anyone. And she wanted to go now, for
she knew when Geoff arrived home, it would be too late
and the gates would be locked. Obligated, she asked Monica
to come along. At first the woman agreed, but when Val
was ready to leave, she changed her mind. Ryan was complaining of a sore throat and she had promised to take him

to the mall later that day. She still would take him if after an hour or two she was convinced he wasn't coming down with anything.

When Val went out to her car, her conscience pricked her. What if something happened to her while she slipped off to do what she desired in private? Though Monica had invited her to go along to the mall, something in her tone hinted she'd rather have Ryan to herself. Valerie bowed out, knowing Geoffrey would have frowned on that decision too. She remembered too well him saying it meant a lot to him that they get along.

Before going to the cemetery, Val stopped at a local florist for a Christmas wreath and stand, and an arrangement for Karl. After pondering for something witty to say, she simply wrote,

> *MANY THANKS*
> *"Kaylene" Valerie Quinn*

It was the least she could do to show she held no ill will. Then, with a new spring in her step, she continued out to the cemetery. She never noticed that she was being followed—had been ever since she left the house.

Fairhaven was located at the edge of town, up on a hill that overlooked the small community of Cedarcrest. Val carried the tripod and wreath to the tombstone and carefully settled it into the freezing ground as best she could.

The young woman pulled the hood of her multicolor wool anorak over her head in an effort to keep out the biting wind. Her eyes swept toward the sky, which was becoming more overcast. The weatherman had said it would snow by evening. Perhaps even sooner, she thought, if the rapidly dropping temperature were any gauge. Val's attention shifted from the pewter-gray skies to the granite stone at her feet.

PATRICK QUINN
BORN SEPTEMBER 9, 1943
DIED DECEMBER 26, 1973

Tears clouded her vision for a moment as she thought about the amiable Irishman everyone seemed to love except the one who should have—her own fiery-tempered mother.

Stooping down, she reached out and touched the cold face of the simple stone. She'd read in Geoffrey's book that if you were hurt by someone who was no longer around, imagine they were in front of you and talk to them. Talking about this thing was long overdue and she really didn't need Geoff to tell her she had to vent these pushed-down and bottled-up feelings. Now was her time and she chose to do it at his graveside.

"Yesterday, Karl Saget told me you didn't start that fire after all. I always knew in my heart that you couldn't have, regardless of what the others were saying. But now at last, I have verbal confirmation of that fact and I want you to know it."

Her eyes shifted over to the other name on that gray, rose-etched stone.

KAY MARLENE QUINN
BORN MAY 17, 1944
DIED MAY 2, 1990

"How I wish the two of you could have worked out your differences. Daddy, I know you must have loved Mom once. But she wouldn't reciprocate that love and your heart turned toward Mrs. Saget, who did. I'm sure you never intended for it to happen, but two children suffered because of your relationship. Karl has long since gone on with his life and now I'm finally able to as well. I love you Daddy . . . I always will. I just wish things could have been different, that's all.''

Rising, Val wiped the tears from her eyes and stood in reflective silence for a few moments before the bone-chilling wind prompted her to move on. She turned, then froze, her heart pounding like a jackhammer inside her chest.

A man in a blue knit cap stood not more than two yards from her. Where had he come from? And how long was he standing there, listening to her very private monologue? She had never heard his quiet approach. Valerie swallowed hard, fighting back the impulse to run, but rather bravely stood her ground, waiting for whatever was to happen. After all, he could be a harmless mourner, or just someone walking through the cemetery when he spotted her lone figure.

He took a step closer and that's when Val caught a whiff of alcohol. Every fiber of her being flew into instant alert as she searched his scruffy appearance. His sandy beard and black leather jacket presented little likeness, though, to the man in the photograph in the great room. As closely as she was surveying him, he was studying her. He spoke first, and though his voice was low, it held a definite threat of intimidation.

''You shouldn't have done that.''

''Done what?'' she queried, but Val had a good idea what he was referring to.

He smiled sardonically. ''I'm not stupid, so cut the act,'' he warned, taking a step closer.

''I don't know what you're talking about,'' Val insisted as she took a step backward. The heel of her loafer hit the edge of the stone.

"Then I'll refresh your memory. You stuck your friend the cop on me. You shouldn't have done it, Kaylene."

With no forethought, Valerie reached for the tripod at her side. She saw the hatred in his eyes, then the pain as she rammed the legs into his abdomen.

He swore, and lunged, knocking the makeshift weapon from her grasp. Val caught her breath, then turned and raced back to the car she'd left parked at the edge of the one-way drive. He was coming after her, she could hear his footsteps pound over the frozen earth, but his movements, luckily, were slowed by the alcohol in his system.

Why had she come here, alone? *Why?* she questioned after the fact, as she slid behind the wheel of her car and locked the driver's side. Val unzipped her shoulder bag and felt about for her keys, but came up with a necklace and a pen. Frustrated, she dumped the contents out on her lap.

Comb . . . wallet . . . compact . . . checkbook . . . keychain! Scooping it up in her left hand, she tossed the rest of the contents back into her still-open purse. Valerie glanced up at the rearview mirror as she was doing this.

He was nearly at the door!

"Oh, no!" Her hand shook as she tried to separate the desired key from the rest. And just as she inserted the key, the man's hand gripped the door handle.

"Open it!" he ordered, smacking the window with the palm of his hand. "I wanna talk to you, Kaylene! Open the darn door!"

The engine roared to life and Val shifted from park to drive. The nearly out-of-control man held on for a second, then let go, but even with the windows closed and putting distance quickly between them, she could hear his imprecations. Her frightened eyes shifted for a moment to the side mirror. He was standing there, shaking his fist at her. Her attention came back to the road, but not quickly enough.

The melting snow across the bend had frozen to rink-smooth ice. She knew she was traveling too fast to make the corner and though she turned the wheel, the car kept heading straight.

The dark shape of a maple tree loomed directly in her path. A dozen thoughts crowded her mind in that second of time . . . but perhaps the most frightening was of her stalker finally getting to her when she was broken and bleeding and unable to run.

Valerie felt the sickening crunch as the hood met the tree and folded back like an accordion. Her body, always strapped in by a safety belt except for today when she really needed it, was flung against the wheel, then slammed backward. Her arms raised instinctively upward in an effort to protect herself from the potential of flying glass.

Then the eerie quietness seemed almost as deafening as the racket of the initial crash.

The young woman sat there, stunned for a few moments. Her head was still back against the neck rest when she heard someone trying to get the door open. Her heartbeat accelerated as she sat statue-still, like a rabbit cornered by a stalking hunter.

The rattling at the door ceased almost as soon as it started, and Valerie blew out a long sigh of relief. He gave up, she thought. At that instant, the unlocked passenger door was swung wide open.

Val cried out, pressing her body as far from the invading arms as she could. "No, Adrian! Please don't!" she pleaded. But the man didn't listen and when his hands touched her shoulder, she slipped into the faint of one eager to escape her living nightmare.

Chapter 12

Gilbert was only a block away when the call came in about the accident up on Fairhaven, but he didn't know Val was involved until he saw her car. A small group had gathered by then and one of the spectators told the officer that a jogger had walked the victim over to the sexton's home where she could wait more comfortably until help arrived.

Valerie walked. . . . *Good*, he thought. *Then she's not in as bad a shape as her automobile*. Gil asked if any of the dozen onlookers had seen what happened. It appeared no one had.

After calling for a flatbed from his patrol car, he requested assistance at the site. Within minutes, he was driving back down the hill to the sexton's old brick home. A middle-aged woman in a wash dress and bib apron answered the door.

"Come on in, Lieutenant. I take it you're here to see the young lady."

Gil confirmed he was as he stepped into the living room, which hung heavy with aromas of frying sausage. When he turned to the woman, he hoped his anxiety wasn't evident. "How is Miss Quinn?"

"More shaken than anything, I'd say. She wouldn't allow us to phone for an ambulance. Insisted she's okay. But she did agree to a cup of tea and is resting now."

"The jogger that brought her down, did he stick around?"

The words had just left his mouth when a young man in a gray sweat suit walked into the room. Gil recognized him immediately—Ted Johnson, a volunteer fireman. As they exchanged friendly greetings, their hostess excused herself to continue with her supper, and Gil came right to the point, asking what happened.

"I'm not sure. I was rounding the corner at the brow of the hill when I heard this commotion. Some guy was trying to get at Miss Quinn, who was in the car. He was pulling on the door when she floored it. She must have hit an icy patch, lost control, and smashed into the elm."

"What happened to this character?"

He shrugged. "He saw what happened and lit out, pronto! I didn't know if I should try to tackle him or help the young woman. I settled for the latter, but it was obvious to me that she was scared half out of her wits. She must have thought I was the same one that was chasing her."

"Did she say anything?"

"Yeah. 'Adrian, please don't.' I touched her and she passed out."

"Adrian?" Gil looked at him hard. "Are you sure?" The witness nodded mutely, then Gil asked him to describe the unknown man.

"Well, now." Ted ran a thoughtful hand across his chin. "I didn't get a really good look, understand. It all happened pretty fast and I was a good distance away."

"Just tell me what he looked like from your vantage point."

"He was rough and unkempt. He had a light beard and a knit cap over his ear-length hair . . . black leather jacket . . . jeans. He appeared to be on the slender side." Now Ted looked hard at his acquaintance. "You think you might know him, don't you."

"Yes." Gil forced a smile. "Thanks for taking the time to get involved, Ted. But then, knowing you, it would surprise me if you hadn't."

"This Miss Quinn . . . she's a friend of yours," Ted said rather than asked.

Gil nodded. "We go back a few years. I think that's it, Ted, at least for now. If I need you, I know where to reach you. Oh," he interrupted when the man began to leave. "Where is the young lady anyway?"

"In the parlor." Ted nodded to the closed door. "She wanted to be alone."

They said their good-byes, then Gil walked into the room unannounced. With the curtains drawn and the late afternoon upon them, the parlor was dark and gloomy. Still, Gil could make out the lonely figure on the overstuffed chair. She'd been sitting forward, her elbows on her knees, her face buried in her hands, but when she heard the door open, she looked up.

Without a word, Valerie rose, letting the afghan that covered her drop back on the chair, and went to Gil's opening arms. As he held her tightly, he could feel her tremble.

For a moment, neither said anything, then she tilted her head back and looked up into his shadowy face. "It was him, Gil. It was Adrian."

"I know. Ted's description matches that of Simmons." He took her face in his hands and looked into her frightened eyes. "Honey, what in the world am I going to do with you? You acted very foolishly by coming here alone."

"Please, Gil, I can't take any of your I-told-you-so right now."

"And you won't hear it, especially since you know my feelings on the matter. I'm going to call headquarters now and get an APB out on Simmons, then I'll take you back to Stoneybrook."

The couple arrived at the estate to find a note propped against a bowl on the foyer console table. Val picked it up and read the scrawling hand.

> *Ryan and I have gone to the mall and we'll have supper there. I took one of Madelyn's chicken corn pies out of the freezer for you and Geoffrey.*
>
> *Monica*

"I'm not leaving you here alone," Gil said, unzipping his jacket. Neither his tone nor his expression left it open to debate. "Did you notify Faraday?"

"No. It's not an emergency. Besides, I'm sure he has emergencies of his own to be taking care of this afternoon."

"Excuses, excuses. Why is it, Val, you can never be open with this guy? You couldn't tell him about your past until you were forced to. When are you going to tell him about the car . . . when he asks where it is? I assume that he does know it's back from the garage."

"And now I've totaled it."

"Things can always be replaced. You can't," he said more gently, looking her directly in the eye. "Are you sure you don't want me to take you to the hospital for a checkup?"

"I'm okay, really. The only thing that's been shattered through this is my nerves," she assured him, ignoring the throbbing in her knee and the aching in her chest. "I don't mean to tell you how to do your job, but I think a better use of your time would be to go after Adrian. Who knows, he might be having thoughts of skipping town."

"When I called the station, the chief said he was sending someone out to his place. They're probably taking him into custody as we speak."

"One can only hope." She slipped out of her heavy anorak and hung it up in the closet. Gil declined her offer to take his and laid it over the chair by the phone. Then he followed her into the great room and sat on the sofa beside her.

"Val, I can understand your desire to go to the cemetery, but what I can't understand is why you went alone. I thought I'd made crystal clear to you the danger you'd be placing yourself in."

"You did, but I thought, what difference can a couple of minutes make? I wanted to do what I had to do in private."

"Leave a wreath?"

She turned on the seat to face him now and her sad expression brightened as she reached for his hand. "I had to tell Daddy the good news and I wanted to tell him alone. Gil, I read Karl's letter last night, and he told me my father was innocent of causing the fire. Karl's aunt accidently started it and she withheld the truth until she was on her deathbed a year ago. I always knew in my heart that Daddy couldn't have done such a terrible thing, but I could never prove it. Until now."

"Oh Val, that's great news!" Impulsively he brought her hand to his lips and kissed it. She drew back, her smile fading as those old insecurities came flooding back.

Gil cupped her chin with his free hand and forced her to look at him. "Listen to me, Valerie Quinn. There isn't one inch of you that repels me, and this notion that you have that your hands are disfigured is utter nonsense. The scars are faint, but even if they weren't, it wouldn't bother me in the least. Nobody's perfect, it just happens your imperfection's visible. Mine aren't."

"Oh?" She lifted a curious brow. "What's your imperfection?"

"I'm impulsive and stubborn. And Dad's told me all my life I've been a sore loser."

"Those are not imperfections."

"Glad you think so. Pam found those traits irritating."

"I'm not your fiancée."

"Not yet. But until you say 'I do' to that baby doctor, you're fair game."

"I take that back. Being stubborn is an imperfection I'm not sure I could live with. Can't you ever take no for an answer, Gil?"

His expression grew serious as the happy-go-lucky side of his personality wore thin. "I'm crazy about you, Valerie. When are you going to open your eyes to the fact that I love you?"

"You're in love with the memories of your past."

"And you're in love with symbolism . . . a handsome doctor who treats sick little kids. And what young woman wouldn't be impressed! But honey, have you ever thought through what he sees in you?"

"Gilbert!" she exclaimed, deeply offended.

"Now let me explain," he cut in, knowing she was jumping to wrong conclusions. "I have thought about it and I believe he wants you for all the wrong reasons. He sees you as a trustworthy and safe stepparent for that wild little cowboy of his. And for himself, he sees a woman who reminds him of his dead wife in so many ways. You're both business women who deal with beautifying the home.'' He reached for the photograph of Jessica and her brother and forced it into Val's not-so-willing hands. ''Go on, take a look, take a really good look. You resemble this woman so much, you could be her sister. You've got her same color hair, even her same hair style. Whose idea was it to wear it long and wavy? You weren't wearing it so sophisticatedly when our paths crossed again last summer.''

The young woman sat there, staring numbly at the photograph, but said nothing. Whose idea was it? Was the thought placed subconsciously in her head when she saw that large picture in Geoffrey's room on his initial grand tour of Stoneybrook, or had he said he bet she'd look attractive with her hair worn that way? She did recall that he told her never to cut it.

''I know the facts are hard to face, but how is it going to make you feel when he takes you in his arms and fantasizes about his first wife. He might even whisper her name unintentionally in your ear in a moment of passion. That would crush you.''

Valerie slid forward and sat the picture back. ''You're also crude. Add that to your growing list of 'imperfections.' A better phrase, though, would be character flaw.''

The door opened at that point and they turned to see Geoffrey enter. His brow puckered in displeasure when he saw Gilbert. ''I thought I heard voices. Lieutenant, what brings you here?''

Valerie rose cautiously. ''Lieutenant Ellis was just leaving. He didn't want me to be alone.''

''Alone? Where are Mother and Ryan?''

''They went to the mall.''

''So, it's the classic case of the fox guarding the hen-house,'' Geoffrey said with a knowing, sardonic smile. ''Thank you, Ellis, but I'll take over from here.''

''Valerie had an eventful afternoon and I think she'd better tell you about it,'' Gil urged, giving her a verbal push.

''Not now.''

''What is it?'' Geoff asked, loosening his paisley tie for comfort. ''Valerie?'' he prodded, his curiosity rising. ''Why is Ellis here?''

Her reply was scarcely more than a whisper. ''I totaled my car.''

''You what?''

Val lifted her hands in an imploring gesture. ''No need to be alarmed, Geoff. My nerves are still a bit shaken, but other than that, I'm fine,'' she assured him, downplaying her very real aches and pains. ''Lieutenant Ellis was kind enough to bring me back and wait until you arrived.''

''Why wasn't I notified about this?''

''She didn't want to disturb your busy schedule,'' Gil offered.

''That's ridiculous. You've misplaced your priorities, Valerie, if you put my practice ahead of your welfare. My associate would have covered for me. As it turned out, we had a fairly easy afternoon.'' He surveyed her face and posture, looking for signs of discomfort, and saw them.

''I still think she should be checked over,'' Gil said, ''but she refused to let me take her over to the hospital. Maybe you'll have better luck.''

''Gilbert . . . '' Val began, a warning tenor in her speech, but Geoffrey cut in.

''For once I agree with you, Ellis.'' Then he turned his attention back on a scowling Valerie. ''I take it you were alone when you had your accident?''

She nodded mutely, thinking this would be the match

which would light the tinder box. Her assumption was right. "Val, you know perfectly well you were not to be driving the streets by yourself. I could expect this kind of irresponsible behavior from Ryan, but not you. What on earth were you thinking of?"

"That's telling her, doc," Gil said with an almost wicked glint in his eye. He couldn't help himself.

As for Val, she bristled, her eyes shifting to meet the lawman's. "I really do think it's time you leave. Now." Then she added, verbally striking back at him, "and since you're so insistent on me being examined, Geoffrey might as well do it."

That wiped the somewhat overconfident smile off his face. "Why? He's a baby doctor."

Geoffrey found that remark offensive. "My practice does consist of more than babies. And I'm sure if Valerie were to have a fracture, heaven forbid, I'd be knowledgeable enough not only to locate it but to treat it as well."

"I know, but . . . but Val's a woman," Gil said, feeling more foolish by the second. She was a woman whose life he was trying to protect so eventually this fellow could marry her! His cheeks reddened at the thought and he was saved from saying something even more foolish by the sound of his beeper. Excusing himself, he asked permission to use the phone.

When Gil returned from the hall extension a few minutes later, he found the silent couple sitting on the sofa, apparently deep in thought. "They've taken Simmons into custody."

This pronouncement startled Geoffrey. "Adrian arrested? What on earth for?"

"Oh, that's right, doc. In the midst of all this confusion, we neglected to tell you what had initially caused Val's accident. Simmons approached Val in a threatening manner up on Fairhaven. She hurried to her car, and in her haste to get away, she slammed into a tree.''

''I don't understand. Why would he want to get to Val? He has no quarrel with her.''

''No, but he does with you. Perhaps he feels you took Stoneybrook from him, so he'll take something from you. Valerie.''

Rising, the pediatrician appeared in deep thought for a moment before walking over to Gil. ''Val told me last night about Adrian being present the night of the fire. So he is aware of her past, and I know he does resent me deeply. If I didn't have Ryan, I'd probably have signed Stoneybrook over to him. But I do have a son and I know Jessica would want him to someday inherit his great-grandfather's estate.'' He shook his head in denial. ''Still, I cannot believe he'd do something this mean-spirited. I just can't.''

''Your brother-in-law owns a garage, doesn't he?''

''That's right. Why?''

''The person who shot Val was driving an old model, American made, dark green pickup with the license ending with the numbers 26. Conway found a dark green truck in Simmons's lot with the number STN 4 26. There's also an unregistered handgun in the glove compartment with a bullet missing from its chambers.''

''You think Adrian took the truck that night?''

''Given the facts, what do you think?''

Geoffrey didn't answer. He couldn't. It hurt him to think it was Jessica's brother who had done this to Val. It made him angry at himself too, that he hadn't suspected Adrian when Valerie pointed out her suspicions. And it embarrassed him that he was so quick to falsely accuse her father for bringing on this entire mess at a time when he wanted no bad publicity. Funny, he'd scarcely given that Chief of Staff position a thought these past couple of days. It didn't seem quite so important now.

Gil walked over to Val and unashamedly caressed her cheek. "It's over, Val. We've got our man, so you can stop being a prisoner now. Go back to your apartment and begin living your life again. Start catching up on your work load tomorrow. I'll keep you posted on how the case is progressing."

Geoffrey watched this man critically . . . this one person who he felt could be a threat to his personal life. He didn't appreciate the familiar way Gil was touching Valerie, or the way she was permitting it. Relief and gratitude were evident on her face, but there was something else too. Geoff stepped forward.

"I appreciate you looking out for Val's safety, but now it's my turn to look after her physical well-being. We keep minimizing the fact that she's been in an accident. And as much as we'd both like her to, she will not be able to resume normal activities tomorrow. Maybe nothing was broken, but she will be plenty sore. Believe me, I've seen enough accident victims to know how these things work." His hand settled on Val's shoulder and he drew her back from Gil's reach.

"Maybe Faraday's right," Gilbert reluctantly conceded. "Maybe you won't feel like doing more than lounging around for a day or two. But I will keep you informed. I'm going directly to the station to talk to Adrian. Perhaps I can get a confession out of him."

"Try not to resort to any arm twisting in your haste to close the case," Geoffrey cautioned.

Now Gil's eyes shifted to the physician. If there was any arm he'd like to twist, it was this man's—right off Val's shoulder. But when he spoke, his quiet tone belied his feelings. "I don't operate that way, doc. Though patience isn't one of my strong points, persistence is. You'll do well to remember that."

Geoffrey's vague smile faded as he watched the officer leave. His glum thoughts were interrupted by the heavy sigh of the woman beside him. He looked at her, evaluating her condition as he unbuttoned the long sleeves of his maize-colored shirt and began to roll them back. "Go to your room and change into something loose."

"Why?" she asked, lifting a suspicious brow.

"Because I'm going to examine you."

"That isn't necessary. You see, I was only trying to get Gil's goat when I suggested that you check me over. I'm okay, really."

But he didn't succumb to her placating smile. "Val, my wife died perhaps because I wasn't aware of any symptoms to alert me to trouble. I don't know that for sure, of course, but this I do know. I never want to have nagging doubts hanging over my head again about a patient under my care. So be cooperative and give me some peace of mind about this, won't you?"

Fifteen minutes later, he began his examination, and though he was gentle, Val thought every area he touched hurt. Especially her knee. She didn't realize, until she'd stiffly climbed out of her slacks and slipped into her over-sized sleepshirt, how bad it looked.

"It's swollen. You must have rammed it against the ignition key," he commented, but was silent as he removed the dressing from her arm and began to snip away at the stitches. Geoff wiped over the area with a ball of alcohol-saturated cotton, then repositioned her garment back over her shoulder and she buttoned the eyelet jabot up to her neck.

"There," he said, snapping his satchel shut, "that wasn't so bad. I'm going to get an ice pack for that knee, then we'll share some conversation over your favorite nighttime beverage.''

Geoffrey returned a short time later with a tray. He helped Val into a sitting position, then adjusted the ice pack over her knee. Lastly, he pulled the wing chair to the bed and sat beside her.

Valerie drew the quilt up over her white cotton shirt. "I'm really sorry about this, Geoff. Had I only stayed here and not gone running off the way I did.''

"Don't feel too badly, for there is another side of the coin, you know," he said, passing her her steaming mug. "Had you not gone out, then Adrian wouldn't have gone after you. Evidently he was watching for the time when you'd be alone and vulnerable. Thank heaven he's caught!''

"I'll drink to that," Val said lightly as she took a cautious sip. "You made this sweeter than usual.''

"I did go heavy on the marshmallows. Sorry. If you can't drink it, I'll make another cup.''

"No, don't bother. This'll do.''

He took a sip from his own mug and glanced toward the drawn curtains. "When I was in the kitchen, I turned on the floodlights. It's beginning to snow. I hope Mother and Ryan return soon because it won't take long for the roads to become treacherous, especially at these dropping temperatures.''

"I hope you're not called out tonight.''

"Me too. I want to stay right here and look after my favorite patient. How are you feeling?''

"Sore . . . very sore," Val confessed sheepishly. "I knew I wasn't in as good a shape as I was leading you to believe.''

"Shame on you, Val, but for the record, you didn't fool me for a minute. I knew you were hurting.''

She returned his smile, took another sip, and leaned back against the pillow. He went on, "I've arranged for the minister to stop by tomorrow at noon. We can't have him meeting you for the first time on our wedding day, now can we, and . . . '' He broke off, noticing that her smile was vanishing as he talked. "What is it?"

"I was just thinking Geoff, now that Adrian's been caught, there's no need to rush into this."

"Everything's set in motion, Valerie. We've had our blood tests, we have our license, and the minister is kind enough to squeeze us in before officiating his Christmas Eve service."

"Squeeze us in? Geoffrey, this is our wedding ceremony we're talking about, not some . . . some doctor's appointment," she stammered. "I always dreamed of walking down the aisle of a chapel, dressed in a long white gown and veil."

"I know." He took her hand and stroked it. "I look back on my big wedding with Jessie and the country club reception which followed. I tend to forget sometimes, that you look forward to having yours too, and believe me, I don't want to deny you having that experience. There's no reason we can't repeat our vows in the spring and have the kind of wedding you've always dreamed of just prior to leaving for Paris."

She withdrew her hand from his light clasp. "It wouldn't be the same, Geoffrey. Our marriage would have already been consummated and the newness would be gone. Besides, by then I might even be pregnant."

"Oh, I hope so! I'd love to have a daughter, and if we do, I hope she has auburn hair just like you."

And Jessie, Val thought wanly, haunted very much by Gil's words. "I want children, Geoff, but I think we should wait a year. Marriage is a big adjustment to make, and in our case, it will be harder because there's your son to consider . . . not just you and me. I'm not sure he's ready for another little person to compete for your affection.''

"There's plenty of that to go around," he assured her. He watched as she took another sip, and thought by her expression that he wasn't doing a very good job of convincing her. "Val, I realize you've been through the crucible these past few days, so to speak, but that's all behind us now. You'll never be in want of anything; after all, my income is in the six figures. If you should find that this house has too many negative memories, we can . . . " he broke off, watching her yawn. "Val, are you falling asleep on me?''

"I'm afraid so.'' She handed him her cup before she dropped it. "Funny, I never thought I could the way my knee was hurting. I guess the ice pack and hot chocolate did the trick.''

His smile was vague as he rose. "I guess so, but then, I knew what you needed. You close your eyes and get some sleep. I'll be in later on to check on you.''

"Valerie? Valerie, can you hear me? Val?'' The voice persisted, pulling her back to awareness.

The young woman forced her heavy eyelids open to find Geoffrey leaning over her. His expression was pinched with anxiety. "What is it, Geoff?'' Her voice sounded strangely thick in her own ears and her tongue felt stiff. What was wrong with her?

"The hospital just called. Ryan was running through the mall when he fell and fractured his arm in two places. I have to sign papers for them to operate. I must go to him, Valerie, I have to help Mother calm my boy. Do you understand what I'm saying?''

"Of course I do.'' She rose up on her elbow and would have tumbled out of bed had he not been there with ready arms to catch her. The room swirled and for a moment she felt as though she were on an amusement ride.

"I'm sorry I disturbed your sleep," he apologized, laying her back against the pillows. "You probably would have slept clear through till morning, but I didn't know that for sure. Had you awakened and I weren't here, it might have alarmed you."

"Geoffrey . . . !" She clutched wildly at his forearms. "Why do I feel like this? Maybe . . . maybe I did bump my head and just don't remember. Take me along to the hospital with you."

"No, Valerie, you're all right. You didn't hurt your head. I examined you, remember?"

"Then why do I feel . . . " It hit her at that moment. The hot chocolate had more than marshmallows in it. She groaned, feeling a sharp sense of betrayal. "Oh, Geoffrey! You know the way I feel about tranquilizers and sedation."

"You needed it, or you couldn't have slept." He easily disengaged himself from her weak grip. "I have to go to Ryan now, but I'll return just as soon as I can. You'll be all right," he promised before his lips brushed her forehead. And with that, he turned and left.

Val lay there fighting the sleep that wanted to overtake her. Geoffrey didn't ask if she wanted to be tranquilized. He didn't, because he knew she'd refuse. Very cautiously, she rose up on her elbow and waited for the room to stop spinning. She had to fight the drug and concentrate on something. Ryan. Yes, she wanted to find out just how badly Ryan was hurt. With this in mind, Val reached for the phone to call the hospital.

But the woman on the other end assured her that no Ryan Faraday had been brought to the hospital that evening—nor was any little boy scheduled for emergency surgery. A chilling hand of fear clutched Valerie in the pit of her stomach.

Even in her drowsy state, she understood what was happening. Geoffrey had been purposely lured away!

Gilbert sat in the living room, stared at the unlit tree, and munched on the last wedge of not-so-fresh shoofly pie. His thoughts were not on the food, nor on the dog whose back he was absent-mindedly stroking. Something wasn't right. When he took Simmons into the interrogation room, he felt he had the guilty party in custody, but when he left, he wasn't so sure about it. Adrian would only admit to being in the cemetery and confronting Valerie, but he insisted he never drove to the Baxter residence in that old truck and shot Val in the parking lot. Gil could usually sense when someone was lying and there was something about Adrian's insistence which warned him not to be too quick to close this case.

"But if it's not Saget, and it's not Simmons, then who is it?" he wondered aloud. "If I have the wrong man, Brutus, that means the stalker's still out there and Val is being lulled into a false sense of security. Maybe I should warn her of that possibility. What do you think?"

The dog barked, and Gil smiled in spite of himself. "Yeah, me too. I'll give her a buzz."

He'd just reached for the phone when it rang. It was Val. She sounded agitated. His concern for her well-being heightened even more when she related the bogus phone call from the hospital. He broke into her nervous chatter.

"Val, sweetheart, listen to me. Get out of the building as quickly as you can. Go into the woods behind the house and don't come out until you're sure it's me. I don't have the patrol car here, I'll be driving my own, and . . ."

"Gil!" she screamed into the receiver. "I hear something. Oh my gosh, I think someone's in the house!"

"Is there a lock on your door?"

"There's a key, but I'm not sure where it's at. Hang on, I think it might be in the desk drawer."

"Val, forget . . . " He broke off, hearing the receiver laid down.

Valerie opened and closed drawers, looking for that key which suddenly seemed so important. She paused, though, as she heard a floorboard creak in the hallway.

"Geoff, is that you?" she asked, both fear and hope mingled in her voice.

No reply. Curious, she opened the door a crack, and there she saw the bearded person in the blue parka and stocking cap. Screaming, she tried to shove the door shut, but she hesitated too long and the stalker was inside the room. Almost immediately, she found herself pinned against the wall, unsuccessfully trying to evade a chloroform-filled cloth.

Chapter 13

Gilbert listened to Valerie's screams in growing dread. "Val! Val!" he yelled helplessly into the mouthpiece. He could hear sounds of a struggle, then silence. Gil slammed the receiver down, and not wasting another second, reached for his jacket. "Let's go, Brutus!"

As Gil slid behind the wheel, he began to pray. "Don't let me be too late, God, please! I'll do anything You want if You just spare Val's life." He went on, gripping the wheel, "I'll quit the force and become a minister like Dad. I'll . . . I'll be less impulsive in my personal life," he bargained, not realizing in his frantic state of mind that he was being more impulsive than ever.

The snow was falling thicker now, and as he sped out of town, he cursed the salt trucks for not being out. Common sense warned him to slow down, but he wasn't thinking as rationally as he should. The sum total of his frenzied thoughts was to get to Val as quickly as possible. In spite

174

of all his efforts, the woman he loved had fallen into the enemy's hands once again. Gil didn't ease up on the accelerator as his tires rumbled across the covered bridge. He could feel a loss of control midway through, but miraculously managed not to plow into the historical red structure. Although he avoided hitting the end of the bridge, he did badly sideswipe the stone wall just on the other side. Metal and stone grated loudly, but he didn't come to a stop until his wheels dropped into the covert he knew was there, and couldn't avoid.

As he and the dog got out of the car, he released a few choice phrases, condemning his own stupidity in how he was handling this. He should have called for backup. Why in the name of common sense hadn't he? His procedures, he knew, were worse than those of a panic-stricken rookie. Pulling his scarf more securely about his neck, he started out on foot for Stoneybrook. It wasn't far . . . a mile, perhaps?

Gil was on the lookout for vehicles coming in his direction. It struck him, as he was jogging, that he'd removed his service revolver to clean it and in the excitement forgot to put it back in his holster. Great! How was he suppose to stop this predator, who was no doubt armed? With a verbal request to halt? There was always Brutus. Thank heaven he had had the foresight to bring him along.

A few minutes had passed before Gil became aware of a car coming up from behind. When it drew closer, he stepped out in the center of the road and waved his arms.

"Please, don't be some skittish female," he prayed. His uniform was clearly visible, but these days even that couldn't be entirely trusted. Then there was the matter of Brutus, who wasn't exactly endearing.

His somewhat chauvinistic-sounding prayer was answered seconds later when the driver braked cautiously to a stop. Gil ran over to the passenger's side and ducked his head to see in the window. It was Geoffrey Faraday and the relief on both men's faces was evident. He didn't wait for an invitation to get in.

"I received a bogus call that Ryan broke his arm and was being prepped for surgery," Geoff greeted him.

"I know. Val called the hospital after you left and they said no one was treated by that name. Then she phoned me. While we were speaking, the stalker entered Stoneybrook."

"What! Adrian's in jail, or did some hot-shot lawyer get him out already?"

"He's still there, unjustly, I might add. He's not the one, doc. Can't you make this car go any faster?"

"Only if you want us wrapped around a pole." He glanced at his tense passenger. "Do you think there's a chance she might have gotten away from him?"

He shook his head miserably. "I doubt if she had the strength to fight him off. That accident put her at a decided disadvantage."

Geoffrey mumbled something more to himself than to his passenger.

"What?" Gil asked, looking through the windshield at the fast falling snow. How could time drag on so?

"I said it's not only the soreness from the accident. I sedated her before I left."

Now Gil turned a pair of narrowing eyes on the driver. "You did what?"

"You said you got the guy!" He swore, uncharacteristically losing his composure for a moment. "I took you at your word!"

"Let's not be at each other's throats, Faraday. Instead, let's put our differences aside long enough to work together to reach Val before it's too late. Saving her is our priority. Agreed?"

"Agreed," Geoff complied, swinging cautiously into his lane. And there, along the edge, they saw a car. The driver was reaching for the door. "There he is!" Gil yelled, and jumped out before Geoffrey brought the auto to a complete stop. With a hand catching the closing door, the lawman pulled the stalker out of the vehicle. Brutus stood on alert, ready for any command.

"Spread your legs and put your hands against the car where I can see them," he ordered before looking over his shoulder to the advancing physician. One glance into the car told him Val wasn't crumbled in the back. "Valerie's probably still inside, and," he said, turning to his prisoner, "she had better not have so much as a scratch on her or you're in big trouble, pal."

Gil began to frisk the felon for weapons, and when he ran his hands over the prisoner's body, his breath caught in surprise. "He's a woman, doc!"

But Geoff had realized this before Gil announced it, for he'd recognized the car. With deep sadness the physician pulled off the beard, then removed the dark glasses. Familiar eyes stared back at him. "My gosh, Corinne, why?" Geoff groaned, shocked almost beyond belief.

Gilbert unwisely took his eyes off her for a moment to look at Geoff when he spoke. The next thing he felt was a jolting punch in his solar plexus when Corie hit him with her fist. Doubling over against the car, he commanded Brutus to stop her as she began to run.

Corinne was no match for the dog, and before she knew what hit her, she was lying in the snow, pleading for Gil to call his animal off.

He did, and as he cuffed her hands behind her back, he began to recite the Miranda rights. "You have the right to remain silent. If you give up the right to remain silent, anything you say can and will be used against you in a court of law. You have the right to speak to an attorney. If you so desire and cannot afford one, an attorney will be appointed for you without charge. Do you understand your rights, Corinne Greer?''

"Yes, I understand," she shot back. Wordlessly, Gil ushered her into the festively decorated house and pulled out a kitchen chair. "Sit!"

Her wary eyes shifted to the dog, not sure whether he would knock her into the chair if she didn't comply. Gilbert leaned forward, his hands on the table. "Now, where's Val?"

"I know my rights. I have no intention of talking until I have my lawyer present."

"Why, Corie?" Geoffrey asked, still unable to make sense of it all.

"You're a smart man, Geoffrey, you figure it out."

Discouraged and disgusted, Gil left the pair and hurried upstairs. Rounding the corner he could see into the guest room. He took in the scene before him. An ice pack lay on the floor beside the bed, the receiver rested on the nightstand where it was hastily placed—otherwise, the room appeared orderly. Gil walked over to the phone and called for a car to pick up a female prisoner, then began a brief search to satisfy himself that Valerie was no longer there. He looked under the bed and opened the door of the armoire, half expecting to find her bound and gagged, but didn't. There was little evidence to suggest that she had put up much of a struggle. Then he saw why. A cloth spotted with chloroform lay by the dresser. Not wasting another second, he raced downstairs.

"We don't have the time for guessing games, Corinne," he said, reentering the kitchen. "What have you done with Val?"

"Please," Geoffrey urged quietly, knowing a harsh tone

would get them nowhere with her. She was on the edge, and had to be dealt with, with that in mind. "You're in serious trouble, don't make it any worse. If you cooperate with us, I'll do what I can to help you. The bottom line is, you have nothing to gain and everything to lose if Valerie dies. Can't you understand that?" he finished, placing an urging hand on her shoulder.

Her defiant eyes suddenly pooled with tears. "Oh, Geoffrey, it didn't have to be this way! I certainly didn't want it to be, but you forced me. I always loved you," she went on in a rush of words, "but you never seemed to know I existed. I thought after Jessie died, and I dated her brother, it would make you take notice. It didn't. And when I found myself in trouble and came to you about it, you told me to put the baby up for adoption and suggested that Adrian not marry me." She smiled bitterly, wiping a rolling tear from her cheek. "He not only wouldn't marry me, he wouldn't acknowledge the baby was his. I hated you both for a while, but my attitude changed when I had Amanda and I thought, at last I had someone who truly was mine to love and care for." She shook her head sadly. "Then she died. You weren't honest with me. You didn't warn me she was a candidate for SIDS."

"How could I, Corie? I didn't know it myself."

"Well, you should have! It was your job to know. Then . . . then for the first time, you began to show an interest in me. You took me out to eat and to the movies. I thought my life was actually turning for the better." Her face contorted. "Then *she* came along and tore that hope to shreds."

"What have you done with Valerie?" Gil cut in, urged on by a feeling that if they didn't find her soon, it would be too late.

But she didn't appear to hear him. Her face was twisted with hatred. "I could hardly believe it when I figured out

who she really was. Kaylene Quinn. Both Jessie and Adrian
had told me the story of the conflagration . . . of Karl's
threats to someday get her.'' Her eyes lifted to Geoff's and
held. ''I wanted to castigate you, to hurt you like I'd been
hurt, but I didn't know how. Then, out of the blue, it all
fell into place and I knew what had to be done.''

She looked at Gil. ''It started with you. You gave me
the idea of the disguise. I figured, if you could fool someone
into believing you were a woman, maybe I could fool them
into thinking I was a man. I thought, who would better scare
Valerie than Karl Saget? However, I knew she needed a
little help to trigger her memory. That's why the tape, to
force her back to the past.''

Her eyes turned to Geoffrey again, and the words continued to rush out. ''Because you chose Valerie over me,
I was determined to use her as a means of embarrassing
you. This appointment for Chief of Pediatrics couldn't have
come at a better time. I wanted you to experience how it
felt to come so close to getting something you really wanted,
only to have it snatched away. And when Karl cleared his
name, I threw suspicion on Adrian. That drunken fool! It
had been easy borrowing a vehicle from his garage. I knew
Adrian had an unregistered gun and I knew where he kept
it. I used it on Val and left it in the glove compartment to
be found.''

Gil cupped his hand around Corinne's chin and forced
her to look at him. ''For the last time, where is Val? Is she
still alive?''

''Maybe . . . I'm not sure.''

The frustrated officer straightened up and he looked at
Geoff. ''I'm going to look in the trunk. And for heaven's
sake, if you have any influence over this woman, get her
to talk.''

He had gone out the front door about the time Monica

and Ryan came in the back. "The roads are horrible!" Monica exclaimed, unbuttoning her coat. "A car ran into the stone wall at the covered bridge and . . . " She broke off, her eyes falling on Corie. That's when she noticed Corie's hands cuffed behind her back. "For goodness sake, Geoffrey, what's going on here?"

He told her. They both forgot Ryan's presence until the child walked over to the woman and looked at her somberly. "Did you really do those wicked things to Val, Corie?"

"Go away, Ryan," she mumbled, turning her head. "Go on, get out of here."

Ryan resisted her commands but stayed stubbornly at her side, running his freckled hand up and down Corie's arm in an imploring manner. "Please don't be a bad lady. I like you, and I don't want to see you go to jail. Won't you tell Daddy and me where you put Val so we can get her. Won't you, huh?"

A sob caught in her throat as her eyes shifted to Geoffrey's and she whispered two words.

When Gilbert walked away from the car after a fruitless search, Geoffrey was tearing out of the house. He was carrying a blanket over his arm and he pointed toward the right. "The ruins!" he shouted. Gil broke into a run, hope fluttering within for the first time since he'd arrested Corie.

The two men stood for a moment among the rubble of beams and stones, their eyes searching through the falling snow. "She's wearing a white, long-sleeved sleepshirt," Geoffrey informed him.

Gil flashed his beam around, looking for a white garment in the snow. Nothing was working in their favor, it seemed. "Val?" His voice rang with question as he stooped to brush the snow away from a mound. A pile of rocks mocked him. Geoff kicked around at a likely spot only to uncover a log.

But Brutus' search was more productive. He pawed some snow away to reveal the still form of the young woman.

Valerie lay curled in an unconscious heap where Corie had dropped her. Dropping to his knees, Gil gently lifted her head and shoulders out of the snow and onto his lap while Geoff reached for her pulse.

"Doc?" Gil was afraid to voice his worst fears. She was so still and cold.

"She's alive," Geoff assured him. Without another word the men wrapped her in the blanket, then Geoff scooped her up into his arms and carried her back to the house. They'd just reached the porch when the police car pulled up the lane. "We each have our jobs cut out for us, Ellis. You tend to Corinne; I'll do what I can for Val."

Gil conceded, though he wished he could follow them upstairs and be with his precious Val when she awoke. It would be Geoff's face she would see when she opened her eyes, his hands she would feel helping her through her ordeal. As the door opened, Gil caught a glimpse of Ryan and heard him ask, "Is she all right, Daddy? Is Valerie gonna be all right?"

Heaving a sigh of resignation, Gil turned to face Conway and the advancing female officer. Faraday was right—he had a job to do—arrest the woman who had tried to destroy so many lives.

After Gilbert booked Corinne, he called Alexandra, feeling she should know what had happened to her friends. Then he phoned Geoffrey to inquire on Val's condition; he was told she was conscious and didn't need hospitalization—just rest. Relieved to hear this, Gil went straight home and tumbled into bed, mentally and physically exhausted, but very grateful.

The ringing of the phone awakened Gil the next morning. It was Geoffrey who asked if Gil could come over at his earliest convenience. Geoff didn't explain why and Gil imagined all conceivable reasons. When the physician answered the door, Gilbert thought he looked as though he hadn't slept very well. "What is it? Has something happened to Val?" he asked solicitously.

"Nothing I haven't seen coming for some time. And wipe that frightened look off your face, Ellis, she's okay. We did a lot of soul-searching and we've come to the conclusion we need time apart to reconsider our future together."

"Where is she?"

"Upstairs. Alexandra's with her."

The bedroom door was standing open, so Gil walked in. First he saw Alex packing Valerie's suitcase, then he saw Val. She rose cautiously from the wingback chair she'd been sitting in to go to him.

Very gingerly, he wrapped his arms around her, afraid he'd hurt her bruised body. "You scared the life out of me last night, sweetheart. Are you really okay?"

"I am now that you're here. Take me home, Gil."

But before they left, she embraced Alexandra. "I'm worried about Geoffrey. This is taking a toll. You will look after him, won't you?"

"You bet!" Tears brimmed in Alex's eyes. "Funny, how you think you know someone, then they pull a crummy stunt like this. I haven't told Megan yet—I don't know how. She loved Corie like an aunt." The woman sighed deeply, her thoughts going back to the man she cared so deeply about. "My parents have a big house. I know he'd be welcome to join Meg and me on our vacation in a few days. You don't think it would be in poor taste to invite him, do you?"

"No, not at all. You've always been a close friend, so I think it would be in poor taste not to."

Fifteen minutes later, Gil escorted Val into her apartment. Setting her bags in the corner, he framed her face with his hands and looked into her eyes. She still appeared plenty pale and fragile to him.

"Look, I have a couple of vacation days coming," he said, speaking his thoughts. "And in view of the fact that I've closed this case and there's nothing that needs my immediate attention, I'm sure the chief will give me the time off."

"Sounds good. Maybe tomorrow, you can take me car shopping." She covered his hands with hers and sighed a deep sigh of satisfaction. "It's great to be home!"

Your home is Victorian Rose, he thought optimistically, *and you'll soon realize that*. He gently kissed her on the lips.

Val sneezed, then groaned. "Oh no! Don't tell me I'm catching a cold on top of everything else."

"Little wonder, dozing off in the snow like that. I'll bring my over-the-counter remedies along when I return. Meanwhile, you get some rest."

She nodded, walked to her room, then turned to look at him. "Geoffrey told me it was Brutus who found me half buried in the snow. Give him a hug of thanks for me, will you?"

"I'll bring him back with me and you can do that yourself." He winked. Perhaps now was not the time to tell her how much he cherished her, but he would tonight.

They exchanged shy smiles before Val walked into her room. She stopped short. Surprise was her first reaction, then delight as she thought, *How like Gil to do this*. At some point over the past twenty-four hours, he had placed a Prince Charming doll on her bed. And on its chest, he'd pinned a child's toy police badge.

Gilbert's words echoed in her memory. "Your prince has come . . . you haven't recognized him yet, but you will. You will."

And Valerie knew that time had finally come and she did.